Closure

Elizabeth Rea

Closure

A Kate Jeffers Novel

READERSMAGNET, LLC

For Mum, because I promised and
Bob, because he means the world to me.

ACKNOWLEDGEMENTS

Many thanks go out to the following people: Pano Karatassos, for allowing me to use his name and the name of his restaurant; Ron Marsh, for his knowledge of police procedure; Lanie Beck for her computer expertise; and especially my husband, Bob, for his unwavering support.

Contents

The Abduction

Friday Afternoon

Eddie rode his bike through Wenn Park and waved to the two boys who were playing on the slide. He knew who they were, but they were just little kids—only six. Eddie wanted to find someone his own age, but didn't see anyone else. He parked his bike next to the wooden jungle gym and climbed to the top to get a better view.

Eddie liked to stand up on top. In the summer he could be up there and no one could find him because the leaves on the surrounding trees were so dense. It was as though he had his own private fort. In the spring and fall he liked the tower on the jungle gym because he could see a long, long way. He pretended he was the captain of a ship out on the ocean. In winter, Eddie could see everything! He often thought of himself as a frontiersman, trudging his way west from mountaintop to mountaintop.

Summer was gone and now the days were getting a bit cooler, so when the wind picked up, he felt the chill. He untied the sweatshirt from around his waist and put it on. He was thankful his sister, Janie, had handed it to him as he rushed out of their driveway.

As he stood on the tower looking out over the park, a car pulled to the nearby curb and someone got out. The person started up the path toward the jungle gym. Eddie squinted, trying to see who it was, but the person's face was shaded in the afternoon sun by the remaining orange and yellow leaves.

"Hi there, Kiddo."

"Hey!" Eddie replied and he smiled when he recognized the voice.

"Come on."

"Where're we going?" Eddie asked.

"I'll show you. It's cool."

Eddie climbed down and followed to the car. The two left Wenn Park and headed east toward Piedmont Avenue. After a brief time, the car turned south onto Monroe Street. Eddie began to get curious.

"Where are we going?" he asked again.

"It's a warehouse," was the reply. "I need to check something out—*and* we're going to play a prank on your mom and dad. Kind of like hide and seek."

"My mom doesn't like pranks…and anyway, I'm supposed to be home pretty soon."

"Don't worry; I'll let them know what's going on."

They turned into the driveway of a big, beige stucco warehouse and parked. Eddie followed to a side door and they both went inside.

"Here's the office," the man said, indicating the door on the right. "You'll be safe and comfortable here till I get back. But I want you to stay right here—you can't go wandering around. There are pallets stacked everywhere in the main warehouse. It could be dangerous. Here," he added, tossing a small bag to Eddie. "There are some chips and a juice box in case you're hungry."

"But we're supposed to eat before too long. Mom'll kill me if I spoil my appetite.

What time is it, anyway?"

"It's not even 7:00 yet. Hang in there, kiddo. You don't have to eat anything unless you get hungry. It shouldn't take them very long to find you. We'll be out of here in no time. Now, stay put. I'll be back soon."

Eddie watched as the office door closed. He heard the lock click into place. It was his first indication that something wasn't right.

CHAPTER I

Kate

Friday Night

At age seven I realized that I was going to have to be careful about using my "gift". Marcie, a girl in my class, came into our room one Friday complaining that she'd lost her birthstone ring.

I've never been tolerant, even as a kid, of whiners, so when I'd had all I could stand, I said, "It's in your closet. Look inside a box… or…something on the floor. You must've dropped it in there."

I wanted to say, 'Check inside your shoe, ya dumbshit. Your ring's in the left one.' But I knew better…for a couple of reasons. One, I figured I'd better not be too specific. I'd give away my secret of being psychic. And two, I'd be in a whole pile of trouble for calling Marcie a dumbshit. Our teacher had no sense of humor!

WELL…That started it! Everyone within hearing distance, including Mrs. Beech, was dead quiet for about ten seconds. The teacher gave me that look…the squinty-eyed, one eyebrow lifted, 'How the heck do you know that?' look and then everyone started talking at once.

By Monday, it was all over school that I'd snuck into Marcie's house and put the ring in her Mary Janes, since she'd run home Friday as soon as school let out. Lo and behold, there sat the ring, just like I'd said.

I didn't need to be a genius to figure out that I'd blown it. Being in second grade, it would be difficult, if not impossible, to explain this so-called gift to "see things" to a bunch of stupid people, (teacher included).

It took me weeks to convince everyone that I'd just made a "lucky guess" and that I wasn't actually a budding criminal. I decided right then that I'd better be very careful with my psychic talents.

At the time I didn't know what to call this gift, and now, years later, I'm still not sure if I'm truly psychic, but for lack of a better term, I think of it that way.

As I went through high school and later college, I knew I needed to find a safe, legitimate way to use my ability. I guess that's one reason I became a cop.

———————

Since you probably *aren't* psychic, I guess I should introduce myself. I'm Kate Jeffers, twenty-five, and I've been working with the police force in Atlanta, Georgia for the past three years. I say 'work with' rather than 'work for' for a very good reason. When I first became an officer, I was buff and in shape. But I'm not into working out. It even got to be a joke (sort of) around the precinct.

There was one day, however, when it wasn't funny anymore. I almost got us killed. My superior, who was then *Detective* Douglas Whitaker and I were in the patrol car, heading to the station when a call came over the radio.

"Any officers in the 10th Street area please respond..." We were really close, so I radioed in to let them know we'd handle the call. Doug hit the lights and siren and we sped to the scene. He screeched to a halt and was out of our vehicle in no time! I was still undoing my seatbelt when Whitaker was already half-way down the alley. He was chasing a perpetrator who, it turned out, was armed. The perp was firing shots at Whitaker, as I was dodging in and out of trash cans, trying to catch up.

The male suspect fired at Doug again. He went down, unhurt, but yelled at me to continue the chase. If I could have caught up, I could have taken the guy out, providing his weapon had run out of ammo. But with his head start, there was no way I could chase him down.

Doug radioed for backup which arrived and eventually caught the guy at the other end of the alley. It was a damn good thing they showed up. By the time Doug caught up with me, I was completely out of breath, doubled over, my chest heaving, legs cramping, and had muscles pulled in every direction. It was embarrassing for one thing, but more importantly, I hadn't been able to cover him like I should have. I was mortified! He could easily have been killed!

"Oh God, Doug! I'm so sorry," I wheezed. But apologies weren't nearly enough. An officer's life often depends on his or her partner and how quickly they react in a time of crisis. And I'd let my partner down—big time!

So Whitaker and I, in a calmer moment later, decided I should chase the bad guys by sitting on my tushie and psyching them out. To tell you the truth, I'm just as glad to be off the streets. It's dangerous out there!

It's not that I'm fat or dumpy, or anything like that. I'm not. I *do* enjoy walking. And I know some Tae Kwan Do. We'd had to live through the training at the academy. It's just that I have other priorities—like eating good food and getting up early (to sit and have coffee). And I hate to sweat.

———※———

I live in a loft in midtown Atlanta, and free-lance out of my home most of the time. You may ask, 'How is a cop able to do this?' It's a reasonable question, since police officers make next to nothing for all their hard work! My younger siblings, David and Emily, and I were lucky enough to be raised by our two grandmothers after our parents were killed in a car wreck. Grandmother Jeffers and Grandmother Phelps had quite a bit of money (from Mom and Dad as well as their own, inherited from our grandfathers).

We moved in with Grandma Jeffers after our parents' accident. I was twelve, Dave was ten, and Emily, eight. Grandma Jeffers lived in a huge house on the outskirts of Buckhead. It is a good-sized estate, where our dad was raised.

My brother, Dave lives in the main house now and our grandmother has moved into the gate house. The property has streams, lots of wooded areas and a stable. We missed our parents, of course, and I still have a recurring vision about their accident. But we all loved Grandma and were able to grow up riding horses, chasing through the woods, and playing in the streams…when we weren't in school.

During the school-year, we spent the week with Grandmother Phelps, our mom's mother. She lives in the Emory area, near the University. We kids all attended a private school near her home. Gran Phelps' house and yard aren't nearly as large as Grandma Jeffers'. That's probably a good thing. There weren't many distractions, so we *had* to do our homework.

Anyway, the grandmothers were savvy enough to plan for our future. They set up a trust for each of us, paid out in installments at our eighteenth, twenty-fourth, and thirtieth birthdays.

With my first installment, I paid for college and invested wisely. (I hope so anyway. You never know with the market these days!) Last year, when I received the second installment, I bought my loft, had it remodeled and furnished it. I've got a few years before I receive my final installment. Who knows what I'll do with that… Probably invest it for retirement!

My loft is the greatest place. When the realtor showed it to me, it was just a huge storage room at the top of an old office building located at the corner of West Peachtree and 14th. It had a twenty foot ceiling and brick walls. It was hard for me to appreciate the space that first day because there were very few windows and the whole place was dark and dingy. The building had been empty for several years and there was dirt and dust everywhere! I had an allergy attack and was about to run, screaming, out of the place, but Kay Stein, the real estate agent, stopped me. She had a better concept of its possibilities than I.

Kay, a longtime friend, convinced me to meet with Robinson Abrams, an architect she knew. He drew up some plans to give me an idea about what could be done with a loft space. I loved his ideas, so we went from there. Rob and I became really close, if you get my drift, but that's another story. Work was finally finished about mid-July, so I've been living here three months.

My loft has two stories. The first floor consists of my main living room, office, kitchen, and dining areas. The upper story is a half-floor and houses my bedroom and bath, along with a closet and storage areas. Rob did wonders with the space. We decided that the beauty of the loft was the fact that it was one big room, so we left it that way.

We created the different living areas by adding partitions at strategic places. Rob wisely suggested an open spiral staircase as well as skylights and large windows to brighten up the otherwise dim space, and what a difference! Once they were cleaned up, the walls turned out to be the prettiest color brick I'd ever seen!

My "front" door is at the end closest to the interior of the building, nearest the elevators. If you enter the loft through that door, there is a bathroom to the left and a huge closet on the right. The closet doors face out toward the main living area. On the end of the closet, next to the front door, there is another door for a coat closet and even a storage place for my vacuum.

The main closet has an enormous amount of space and that's where I keep all my office stuff. It holds my computer, printer, fax machine, scanner, copier and file cabinets, as well as all my office supplies. I'm not terribly organized by nature, so it really helps to have a specific place for everything. Rob, on the other hand, is extremely detail oriented. He thought of everything!

We put all my office equipment on rollers, so I can pull out whatever I'm working with. My desk backs up to the closet doors and faces out into the rest of the loft. This way I don't have to sit with my back to the beautiful views. Because all the equipment has wheels, I can easily "close up" my office at the end of the workday. A spiral staircase separates the office from the living room. The living room and dining room are both two stories and are brightly lit due to the windows and skylights. On the wall opposite the entry is a fireplace and French doors that lead outside to a brick patio and my container garden.

I find gardening therapeutic. I like to mull over my cases while digging around in the dirt. I find I often have my visions when I'm working with plants. Maybe it has something to do with getting back to basics…to nature. Who knows?

In between the bathroom and dining area is my kitchen. I really didn't mean to leave it till last, but there you have it. I'm not much of a cook. Okay, I can boil water and I also make a mean macaroni and cheese…from a box.

The kitchen is gorgeous and has the most wonderful stainless steel appliances. The granite countertop looks super and ties everything together including the old brick walls. My goal is to learn how to cook really soon—maybe between my next two assignments.

The upstairs area of my loft is cool, too. It covers half the area of the downstairs. Actually, it's a huge balcony overlooking the living and dining areas.

As I walk up the spiral stairs, I can see my bed. To the right are the upstairs bathroom and a space that is a dressing room and closet, combined. Beside the staircase, a railing stretches to either side, and there are two long, skinny storage areas that run the rest of the length of the loft. One is even cedar, so I can store my wool clothes without having to worry about moths. The really cool thing is that the closets practically disappear, so if someone wasn't looking carefully, they'd never know they were there. I'm nuts about my new place. It's close to everything the city has to offer: the theater, Symphony Hall, the High Museum, and several wonderful restaurants, including Pano's Veni Vedi Vici, within walking distance.

At night, when Atlanta is all lit up, I love to sit out on my patio with a glass of wine and look out over the city. I feel safe and secure in my space. I know how evil a big city can be. It's fortunate that I can do a lot of my work from home. I'm basically a chicken.

Well, that's my good news. I've also got some areas of my life that pretty much stink. For one thing, I miss my parents and would like to find out what *really* happened on the night they died. Another thing that sucks is that I'm still single. I've got one guy I'm crazy about, but that's depressing, so I'll tell you about him later. I've been through a few other relationships, but for some reason, when they find out I have visions, they get skittish and call it quits. Go figure! I've finally realized I need to be more cautious in *that* area, too!

Rob, the architect, is the guy I've sort of been seeing lately. He thinks I'm a free-lance detective, and I'm not about to say anything to change his mind.

I had to tell him *something* since he was designing my office. I have a lot of confidential files on many cases, so it's obvious that I'm in the Criminal Justice field in one way or another.

I haven't seen Rob as much lately, since my place has been completed. He *says* he's working on a new project and that it's taking most of his time. I'm not so sure. I have a feeling that he liked my *loft* a little better than he liked me! My friends say I'm being silly, but I can't seem to get over my feelings of insecurity. To anyone who doesn't know me, I appear to have the world by the tail. And yet, I feel inferior in so many ways. Especially when it comes to guys. You'd think I would have some "visions" about this relationship stuff, but it doesn't work that way. Ah, well, life bites on occasion.

Back to being a cop. I got my latest assignment tonight. About 8:15, Whitaker, who is now our lieutenant, called me. I was sitting there, relaxing, when the phone rang. I hate to admit that I was home alone on a Friday night, but it's true. So much for my social life. At any rate, the phone startled me and I was so surprised that I dropped the damned thing and it crashed into a million pieces on the floor! Crap!

I hurriedly grabbed my cell from my briefcase (a huge black bag that I lug with me wherever I go) and returned Whitaker's call. I knew this had to be 'big' for him to call me at home on a Friday night. As soon as I realized what he was saying, I grabbed my keys, headed downstairs to the parking garage, said a quick "Hey!" to Gloria at the security desk, and hustled over to the station to be briefed.

I knew that Glory, as she's called, wanted to talk. She *always* wants to talk!

Normally I don't mind, but tonight I was in a hurry! Actually, Gloria's very nice—quite a live wire and fun to have around. She's in her mid-twenties like I am. But as opposed to me, she is *very busty* and knows how to use her figure to her best advantage. She knows everything that goes on in our building (whether you want her to or not!) and is an uncontrollable flirt.

I asked her once how she happened to work in our parking garage. Turns out, she used to drive for a limo company, but got canned for having a drink (and so forth) with one of her rides. The guy's date got just a wee bit bent out of shape when she caught Glory smooching with her man! Oops!

"Well, if he hadn't been so damn cute, I could've resisted!" she'd said.

But her boss liked her, in spite of her short-comings, and helped her land her current job. I suppose they figured she'd be out of the way, stuck in a parking garage, but it seems that nothing can hold her back!

Thinking about her, I chuckled as I drove to the Midtown Police Station on Monroe Street. It's less than ten minutes from my loft. Very convenient!

Detectives Carlos Williams and Amy Stevens were in the lobby when I arrived. We've worked on other assignments over the past couple of years, so they are used to my visions, thank goodness. There's nothing worse than having to stop and explain things when we should be working a case. Lieutenant Whitaker motioned for the three of us to follow him back to a conference room where he'd already started a new pot of coffee—it didn't take one of my *visions* to figure out this was going to be an all-nighter.

CHAPTER 2

Monroe Street Station

Friday Night

Whitaker began: "Okay, people, here's what we've got so far: Edward Bryant, 8-years old; goes by "Eddie". Disappeared from Wenn Park—right across from his house here in Ansley Park. This was at about 6:30 this evening, according to the parents, who were at home, and two other neighborhood boys who were at the playground. Bike was still there. No one saw anyone suspicious, no one heard anything unusual. Kid was there one minute, gone the next.

"Now, the parents: Arlington and Penn Allister Bryant. Both 40 years of age. One sister: 13 year-old, Janie. Family is well off, influential in Atlanta. The Allisters and Bryants, I'm sure you've heard the names. Kate, you probably know these families socially. That's why we're moving so quickly on this. We're assuming kidnapping, although we can't say that for sure. As I said before, the family was at home when the disappearance occurred. By the time Carlos and Amy arrived at the house, Arlington's brother,

Emerson, was there, too. He'd been invited for dinner. All right, you two," concluded Lieutenant Whitaker as he glanced toward the detectives, "fill Kate in on the rest."

"We arrived at the home, 880 Westminster Terrace, at 7:02p.m.," Amy began, glancing at her notes. "The mother was hysterical, so I took her into the library to talk her down. Carlos went to the sunroom with dad, sister, and uncle. As soon as the black and whites had secured the alleged crime scene, they brought the neighbor boys to the house. Boys had still been playing, unaware that Eddie was gone. Carlos had the kids call their parents to let them know where they were. Then he took the boys' statements, (here are your copies of all the statements taken)," she added passing them out, "and then one of the officers took both boys home."

"And no one heard or saw *anything*," I asked, incredulously.

"Nary a thing," Carlos answered. "Boys were still playing and were surprised to see the cruisers pull up. Keep in mind, however, that the slide on which they were playing is located at the opposite end of the park from where the Bryant boy's bike was found."

We all nodded and gave that a moment's thought. I suppose that it would be possible for the kids not to have noticed anything amiss. I'm familiar with Ansley Park, but not with the park where the boy was allegedly taken. I needed to go there and familiarize myself with it. All that being said, my instincts started yelling, "inside job"! An eight-year-old isn't going to go with a stranger willingly. He's old enough to know to make a big stink if approached by someone. He probably *was* taken, somehow, though. I kept my thoughts to myself, however, and asked only, "When did the family realize that the child was gone?"

Williams responded. "Eddie had gone to the park at approximately 6:15 p.m. The dad had told him not to be gone too long, that his Uncle Emerson was coming for dinner. He also told the boy that Janie'd be over to get him in about half an hour if Eddie wasn't back yet.

"The neighbor boys confirmed the timing, even though neither one had a watch. We're only talking half an hour window, tops."

Carlos referred to his notes again and continued, "According to the sister...uh...Janie...she walked across the street to Wenn Park at 6:45, saw the bike, but not Eddie. She saw the neighbor boys, but only waved to them since they were on the equipment at the east end of the park. She briefly looked around, and then returned home, thinking that maybe she'd missed him somehow, and told her parents she didn't see him. They searched the house and gardens there, and then called us."

Stevens then concluded by saying when she'd gotten Penn Allister calmed down and questioned her, she'd gotten a similar story. The only difference was that Mrs. Bryant, Penn Allister, had been in the master suite, upstairs, dressing for dinner when Eddie left for the park.

CHAPTER 3

Westminster Terrace

❖

Friday Night

It helps me to visit the actual crime scene, but since it was 9:30 and already dark, I didn't think I could get a good feel for the situation at the park. Instead, I told Whitaker I'd head over to the house. He'd informed the family that I'd be working the case, so they wouldn't be surprised to see me. I figured that the sooner I got there, the better; although I didn't think the family would be going to sleep any time soon. Amy poured me a to-go cup, and I took off.

The scene on Westminster Terrace was tense, to say the least. The park had been cordoned off with yellow crime scene tape, and there were two cruisers, one parked at each end. Another car, unmarked, was in the driveway of the Bryant home. I parked out front and struggled up all the steps up to the porch. Man, Atlanta's way too hilly. Or, maybe I just need to make myself exercise. The house was ablaze with lights. An officer I hadn't met (name badge said Gomez), opened the door for me and said the family was in the library. Gomez led the way, and then stationed herself at the desk where the phone had already been wired to trace calls.

I knew Penn Allister by sight. My grandparents had been on the board of directors for the symphony with her parents. We'd been to several functions, charity events, with the Allisters and the Bryants. Penn is about fifteen years older than I and it had been quite a while since I'd seen her. I know this wasn't the best time to assess her, but still, I was shocked. She looked like the devil. She's always taken good care of herself, but tonight her hair, an attractive shade of blonde, was sticking out in every direction, and her usually expertly-applied make-up was in streaks running rivers across her face. Ever the lady, though, she stood and greeted me as soon as I walked in. I hugged her, which brought forth a fresh torrent of tears.

"Penn," I said, handing her a relatively clean tissue from my pocket (it was the best out of the wad I had smooshed in there), "I'm so sorry y'all have to deal with this. I'm here to help if I can, and hopefully we can get to the bottom of this quickly." I nodded to the rest of the family, and sat down on a nearby chair.

The room was lovely, a study in good taste that looked as though it should have been in some home magazine. The walls were painted pale yellow with glossy white moldings, trim and built-in bookcases. In front of the fireplace, overstuffed furniture was grouped for cozy reading or conversation. The chairs and couch were covered in beautiful chintz, some with stripes and others with cabbage roses in pastel yellow and gorgeous shades of red. There were accents of green and white which served to tie the entire room together. Very striking…as I'd expect for such a prominent family.

Arlington was on the couch, his arm around Janie, who appeared to be dozing. He, on the other hand, looked completely wired… really on edge. Emerson, whom I calculated to be a bit older than thirty-five, looked haggard. He was sitting in a wing chair, opposite the couch. He'd lost a bunch of weight since I'd last seen him and his eyes looked glazed over. *Booze or drugs?* I asked myself. I noticed that he was the only one with a drink; bourbon, by the looks of it.

I was about to ask for an update when the phone rang. Arlington Bryant jumped like he'd been shot, jerking Janie fully awake, her eyes big as saucers. Emerson and Penn Allister both sat bolt upright, hands clenched, jaws tight. Officer Gomez motioned to Arlington to pick up the cordless extension on the end table next to the couch. She turned on the recorder and picked up the desk phone at the same time.

"Yes, this is he," said Bryant. He bounded from the couch and began to pace the room. "Of course I want my son back! Who is this? What do you want?"

I *hate* only hearing half the conversation! It makes me nuts. But I figured we'd hear the other side in a minute. So instead I concentrated, watching Arlington. I'm a pretty good judge of character. I can usually tell when someone is putting on an act. And Arlington wasn't.

"Five hundred thousand…where? When? Wait! Let me talk to him. How do I know he's still okay?"

Obviously, Officer Gomez had prepped Arlington. Our collective fingers were crossed in hopes he'd be able to keep the person on the line long enough for a trace.

It wasn't going to happen. The line went dead. Arlington looked at the phone and his shoulders slumped, defeated. All eyes turned toward Gomez.

"Not enough time," she said, shaking her head. "But at least now we know what's going on. This is for real, just like we thought. And since they called this soon, there's a good chance they may still be here in the city."

I wondered if Gomez was *always* this optimistic.

We all listened to the recording. Half a million, delivered to a location at Hartsfield Airport, Tuesday. More specific details to follow. When Gomez played it through again, I concentrated on the voice. It had obviously been disguised. It sounded like a man, although I couldn't be sure. Everyone sat completely still for a minute, in shock, absorbing the details. I walked over to the desk and spoke quietly with Officer Gomez. After a few moments, she addressed the group.

"I'm going to call Whitaker to inform him of the ransom call. Then I'll remain here throughout the night in case they call back. Ms. Jeffers...Kate...will be outside. At daylight she'll check the park and will then report back here.

"I'd suggest you all lie down and at least try to rest even if you *can't* sleep. The next few days are going to be tough on everyone."

I thanked Gomez and the Bryants, said good night, and let myself out. I stood on the porch for a moment, looking around. Eddie had not used this door when he'd left. He'd used the back door. According to the sister, he'd gotten his bike out of the garage located at the back of the property. He had driven down the driveway, located on the right side of the home. The chances are good that he had crossed the street directly in front of the house and had ridden straight down the path to the playground. The sister, Janie, said he usually played on the jungle gym.

I breathed deeply. The night was cool, definitely fall weather. The breeze rustled the remaining leaves on the trees, and I could see leaves swirling around on the ground. The night seemed so peaceful, but there was *no way* I was going to be able to sleep.

Between the coffee and the adrenaline rush I'd had at the sound of the phone, I was jumpy. I sat in my car, surveyed the neighborhood, and pondered.

A half million dollars these days isn't considered that much money. Ansley Park is a great neighborhood: super location near downtown Atlanta, neat bungalow houses, with very deep, but narrow lots. People who live here are well-to-do, but not millionaires. The kidnappers must have known how much to demand, how much the Bryants could come up with in the next four days. Arlington hadn't even blinked when the caller had named the ransom amount. I wondered who was behind this and where Eddie was at the moment. An eight year old kid...what a mess.

I finally leaned my head back on the seat and rested my eyes.

CHAPTER 4

Eddie

———— ● ————

Friday Night

E ddie looked around the room in the warehouse where he was
being kept. There was only one door, solid metal…and it was
locked. There was a big brown desk and chair. On the wall next to
the desk was a bulletin board with some push pins, but no notes.
There were several boxes stacked in one corner. The room looked
like it was supposed to be the office, but besides the furniture, there
was no office stuff.

The guy had turned on both florescent lights that were
suspended from the ceiling. The only window was way, way high
up on the same wall as the door. Eddie supposed it looked out over
the main warehouse. The window looked as though it had a latch
on the bottom that would allow it to swing open. If he could get up
that high, he would probably be able to see the outside door where
they had entered earlier.

Eddie scooted the swivel chair from the desk to the space below
the window. He could tell there was no way he'd be tall enough,

even standing on the chair, so he pushed it back. The desk was out of the question—way too heavy, even to push an inch at a time. Eddie considered the boxes. Some of them would be too much for him, but a few looked small enough. He tried several of the smaller boxes, stacking them on top of one another. Five boxes later, he climbed the stack and tried to see over the window ledge. Almost! He could just peek over the sill. It was nearly dark in the warehouse, but he could make out the silhouette of a large person; not the one who'd locked him in the office. One more box would do it—then he could hoist himself up onto the ledge. If the big guy walked away for just a couple of minutes, Eddie could push open the window and escape!

He was about to climb back down and put his plan to work when the man turned around and saw him. "Wha' do you think you're doin'?" he yelled at Eddie. "Git down offa there!"

Eddie, startled, toppled sideways and crashed to the floor, boxes and all. He scrambled back to the desk and sat, frozen in the chair. He scarcely breathed. His heart hammered. His arm hurt.

"Don't make me come in there, kid!" he heard the man yell through the locked door. His voice sounded scary. "You sit tight and everything will be okay. We'll be getting you some sandwiches and a sleeping bag before too long. Just don't do anything stupid. I don't want to have to hurt you."

CHAPTER 5

Lieutenant Whitaker

———— ● ————

Friday Night

Whitaker walked wearily back the hallway to his office and eased himself into his desk chair. He leaned back and put his feet up on his desk—it helped him think, he said. It had been a tough night already and it didn't show signs of improving.

Williams and Stevens were good at their jobs—the best he had on the force—they'd give it their full attention. But Whitaker had decided to add Kate Jeffers to the mix—and he wasn't exactly sure why.

Kate was just as good at what *she* did. Yes, she had "visions" which made some people skeptical, but they *did* seem to pan out. She had helped break several cases. And she moved in social circles that no one in the department had access to. She'd been a cop, not too good, fitness-wise, but she came through when she needed to.

Cases involving kids always got to Whitaker. The innocents. People were nuts and so often it was the children who suffered. That was another reason to call Kate in. She was an advocate of the underdog, the helpless, just like himself. And he liked her…that was the bottom line. He had to admit it.

He felt guilty thinking about Kate like he did. Margo, his wife, had died four years earlier and he hadn't allowed himself the time or energy to even think about anyone else—it hurt too much. He'd thrown himself more and more into his work. He'd done well and advanced in the department, so he couldn't complain about that. It's just that when Kate was involved in one of their cases, work was easier to handle. He'd even kept her phone number on speed dial in his office. There was something about her—she sparked up the room when she came in. And it *had* been a couple of months since they'd called her in on a case.

Doug was several years older than Kate and she was rich and high-class—even if she *was* self-deprecating at times. He didn't stand a chance!

Whitaker wondered if he was the only one who thought about Kate in this way—and whether she ever thought about him at all. That made him feel guilty all over again. He had loved Margo more than anything. Then she saw him on the street one day and was walking over to say hello—she didn't know he was in the middle of a sting—and BLAM! That was it. He prayed she never knew what hit her. She hadn't died immediately, but hadn't seemed to be in any pain. And her death had been his fault. If he hadn't been a cop, she'd be alive today.

He vowed never to allow himself to put someone in that position again…so he shoved his thoughts about Kate into the recesses of his mind and tried to keep them there.

His phone rang…it was Officer Gomez. They'd guessed right— the Bryant kid *had* been kidnapped. The kidnapper had called the home.

"Well, shit…" Whitaker sighed, removed his feet from the desk and got back to work.

CHAPTER 6

Joey and Eddie

———————●———————

Friday Night

"Here you go, Kiddo," said the big guy, opening the door a crack and handing in a sandwich to Eddie.

"Thanks for the food, but don't call me Kiddo. That's what my uncles call me, and you're not my uncle. I thought we were gonna play a game…like hide and seek…a trick on my parents. This doesn't feel like a game. I want to go home."

"Don't worry, kid. You won't have to stay here much longer. What do you say we play a game of cards or something?"

Eddie peered through the opening in the doorway. "It's kind of hard to play cards when you're on that side of the door and I'm in here. And I don't even know your name."

The man chuckled. "You know, you *are* a funny kid."

"My name's Joey. I think it'd be okay if I came in there with you. Hold on a second. I'll grab a deck of cards and be right there. You want a soda-pop?"

Joey returned with drinks and cards. "I don't know too many games," he mumbled, hanging his head. "Just gin rummy and stuff like that."

"How about 'Go Fish'?" asked Eddie, realizing that Joey probably wasn't terribly smart.

Joey's eyes lighted up. "Yeah…I know that one! Cut for deal."

"What's going on anyway, Joey?" asked Eddie in between rounds. "Why am I here to begin with?"

"I don't know. I work here at the warehouse and Mr.…ugh… someone asked me to keep an eye on you. I need some extra cash."

"You mean you're getting *paid* to look after me? Like a baby sitter?" Eddie was affronted.

"Well, sort of." Joey knew all too well about people thinking he was dumb like a little kid, so he added, "…but you're too *old* for a *baby* sitter."

Continuing, he said, "As I said, I know all about this warehouse. This place can be dangerous…these big, heavy boxes all over the place."

Eddie accepted that remark. "But you got paid?"

"Not yet. We should get a call here by ten o'clock tonight," said Joey, tapping the cell phone in his shirt pocket. "Then I'm supposed to get my money and you can go home."

"Who's paying you?" asked Eddie, eyeing the lump that was Joey's phone and wondering if he could somehow get his hands on it.

"Oh, no. Can't tell you that, kid. You probably think you can outsmart old Joey, but no… If I told you, I wouldn't get paid…

"Uh…whose deal is it, now?" Joey asked, his mind back on the game.

CHAPTER 7

Kate

———— ⬤ ————

Friday Night

I must have dozed for a while, but it was still pitch black when I opened my eyes. I don't think I had fallen asleep, but I'd definitely had a vision.

This one confused me. Always before when I've been on a case, my visions have been quite distinct and very much related to the situation at hand. This one was still a bit hazy and didn't seem to connect at all. I saw someone lying in a fetal position. I couldn't make out a face. It appeared to be a male, but couldn't have been Eddie Bryant—way too big. The person was moaning, as if in pain. Try as I might, I couldn't make out any of the surroundings. I couldn't even tell if he was inside or out.

I sipped my now-cold coffee, wishing daylight would hurry up. Patience has never been one of my long suits.

I closed my eyes again and another vision came to me. These visions are sort of like dreams, but occur when I'm awake as often as when I'm half-asleep. I never know. They are just a whole lot more vivid than regular dreams.

I'd had this particular vision twice before. The first time I had it was when I was twelve, the day before my parents died. It was horrible and I didn't understand it at all. *Why would it come back now?* I wondered.

In this vision, I was in the back seat of a car and my mother, sitting in the front passenger's seat had been singing along with the radio. That always bugged my father who was driving, since my mom had a terrible voice. But I always thought it was funny.

She knew she couldn't sing worth a hoot, so she sang *really* off-key, just to make me laugh. Of course, I obediently did so and urged her on. She turned to look at me sitting behind her and her look changed from one of delight to a look of absolute terror! The color drained from her face, her eyes got huge and focused on something behind me. She let out a blood-curdling scream as I instinctively ducked.

That's it. I always come back to reality at that point.

I remember where I was the first time I had it. I was at band practice and the vision rocked me so hard that I dropped the cymbals right in the middle of dress rehearsal…scared the bejesus out of everyone. I tore through the back curtain on the stage and collapsed on the short stairway leading down to the main seating in the auditorium. It scared me so badly that I wet my pants. They found me in a heap, sobbing uncontrollably, smelling like piddle and shaking like a leaf.

Someone called my dad, who was nice enough to come and get me. I remember him spreading a big, plastic garbage bag on the seat of the car ("Just so we won't have to mess with it later," he'd said), smiling his crooked smile and telling me not to worry.

The band director must've told everyone I had a bladder infection or something, because most people were pretty sympathetic.

In truth, however, I was too embarrassed to go back to band and the sound of cymbals freaks me out to this day.

Anyway, I was never musically inclined…which was why I'd been relegated to playing the cymbals in the first place. Do you suppose I got my talent, or lack thereof, from my mom's side?

———⬥———

This time, the vision had been just the same up until the very end. This time right before my mother screamed, she yelled "Elliot! Look out!"

I jolted forward in my seat, drenched in sweat. I jerked around to see what was behind me that was so horrendous and then realized it had been a vision.

It took me a minute to regain my composure. I dug some nasty tissues from my pocket and mopped my face and neck. I began to talk to myself, in reassuring tones. *No, you're not twelve anymore. You're twenty-five. Your parents are not going to die tomorrow in that awful car crash. That was years ago. You're here, in Ansley Park, waiting for sunrise so you can get back to work on Eddie Bryant's kidnapping case.*

I still often wonder about my parents. Yes, they *had* died the day after my vision. It still creeps me out! But I hadn't been with them. Their car had gone over the edge of the road and down into a ravine. It had flipped, burned and was so badly damaged that there was no telling exactly what had happened. There was some question as to whether there had been another car involved, but the evidence was inconclusive. The police assumed that they had been driving too fast on the slick road and my father had lost control.

I never bought that. My dad had always been a good driver and had never had any kind of accident. As kids we'd gone bonkers because it took *forever* to get anywhere because of Dad's *slow* driving.

I'm convinced that someone ran them off the road that night. I'm sure that's what my mom saw and why she screamed.

I've been gathering information on that night for several years and have a sizeable group of clippings. Articles about their deaths were in all the papers since they'd been so active in the Buckhead social scene. Since becoming a cop, I've been able to get hold of more files. I have a folder in my cabinet on the events that took place that day. I hope some day to prove that they were not at fault. Maybe I'll find out who *was*.

I took a few deep breaths and glanced around my location. Thank goodness the area was empty. If anyone had seen or heard me during the past few minutes, they'd lock me up and toss away the key!

CHAPTER 8

Lou

Friday Night

Lou Mancini sat at his mahogany desk in the upstairs office of his club. The noise from the bar drifted up and he smiled, thinking about the big bucks they were raking in downstairs.

His smile faded when Ronnie walked in. "Boss?" said the very large guy. Ronnie was wearing jeans and a black t-shirt that looked as though they had been painted on.

Lou shook his head. He, himself, was getting a little paunchy—sitting at a desk all the time. Ever since his accident, his back had been giving him trouble. He was in constant pain. It was all he could do, sometimes, to walk. He'd stopped trying to exercise years ago.

It rubbed him the wrong way when he looked at these younger guys, all lean and hard. But hey, screw it. That's why he'd hired these guys. That's what he was paying them for.

And if *he* was intimidated by Ronnie Walker's looks, Ronnie'd sure as hell scare the crap out of anyone else. Besides, Lou was getting too old for the streets. He figured he'd sit back, use his brain and let the younger guys do the rough stuff.

"You're back earlier than I thought you'd be," began Lou. "Did you get the money?"

"No, not yet. There's been a complication—cops are all over the place—now I hear there's been a kidnapping!"

"What the...?"

"Yeah...and now they've called in some psychic chic."

"But I talked to the guy who did it. Says he'll have the money by Tuesday night."

"Right," Lou responded. "I've heard that from him before. And who's this broad that's sticking her nose in?"

"I did some checking. Her name is Kate Jeffers. She's a freelance dick. She's worked with the Metro cops for a while now. They've got her on this kidnapping case 'cause the Bryants are high society."

"Jeffers...Name rings a bell. No matter...I want her off the case. I don't believe in any of this woo-woo stuff, but get her off my back anyway. Do whatever you have to do to make sure she leaves this case alone. I don't want her or anyone else screwing this up—I need that money—I've waited too long as it is!"

"Right. I'll make some calls, Lou. Find out where she lives and so forth."

"You do that," Lou said and waved his hand dismissively. Ronnie left the office.

Jeffers...hmmm, Lou mused, trying to remember why that name sounded familiar. Lou struggled out of his chair and hobbled to the window, rubbing the small of his back. As he looked out over the lights of Atlanta he thought, *Damned accident.* Ronnie reminded Lou of himself when he was a younger man. *Look at me now.*

Lou could still picture that night, years ago, as though it were yesterday. A stormy night, some fog. He and Nick Escoba had been driving up a hilly road, going to one of Nick's favorite clubs—one he liked to frequent whenever he flew in from South America. All of a sudden they rounded a curve and plowed into the rear of a slow moving car.

Nick hadn't even had time to step on the brakes. Lou, however, had reacted by bracing himself and twisting away. That's when he'd felt his back go out. Oh, the pain!

The other car had been pushed through the guardrail and had plunged into a ravine, where it had burst into flames. Nick had driven a little further up the road, parked, and escaped on foot. He would have been deported again if he'd been caught in the States… not to mention what would have happened if he'd been caught driving with no license *and* causing a fatal accident!

Lou had been left in the car by himself, dazed. He wasn't sure how long he sat there, but the sound of approaching sirens brought him to his senses. He'd managed to drag himself over to the driver's seat and go on.

A couple hours later, though, the pain had become so intense that he'd driven himself to Grady Hospital's Emergency Room. He finally was seen, but not for hours. That night had been busy… too many emergencies—mostly gunshot wounds—that needed immediate attention. He thought about going elsewhere, but was afraid he would pass out from the pain before getting anywhere else.

As it was, he'd hit a cement wall as he was pulling into the emergency parking lot. *Good thing,* he had thought at the time. That helped to explain the dent in the front bumper—and there'd been witnesses.

He had never been concerned about the accident—just about his back. But now it was coming back to haunt him. As he stared out the window, he knew *exactly* where he'd heard the Jeffers' name.

CHAPTER 9

The Kidnappers

3:00 a.m. Saturday

The kidnappers looked in on Eddie. He was asleep on the floor next to the desk in the old office of the warehouse. Earlier, Joey had taken in a sleeping bag and pillow for Eddie.

"He's really sacked out. Poor kid, while you were gone, he tried to see out the window by stacking boxes and stuff. As soon as I noticed, I yelled at him through the door. It scared him and he crashed to the floor. Then he just sat at the desk—real quiet-like."

"Good," was the reply. "We don't need to scare him to death, and I sure as hell don't want him hurt! Pretty soon everything should be back to normal. We get the money to pay Mancini off and they can have the kid back."

"Well, I felt sorry for him and was afraid he'd gotten hurt in that fall—he was rubbing his arm when I peeked in the door. So I sort of went in to talk to him."

"You *sort of* went in? Man, you let him *see* you?!"

"Yeah. I really went in," admitted Joey, beginning to feel stupid. "But I could tell he was kinda scared, so we played some cards... It'll be okay. He's a good kid.

"When are we calling again?" asked Joey, happy that Eddie's arm hadn't been badly hurt and wanting desperately to change the subject.

"As soon as it's daylight all the cops should be back at the house. They've got that girl psychic working with them. She's completely stumped. It's real funny to see her standing around scratching her head, trying to look smart.

"Anyway, that's when we should call, when everyone's there. I'm going to write everything down for you, word-for-word, just like last time. We'll practice again, so you'll know just what to say. Then you can make the call while I keep my eye on things at the house.

"Everything's going right according to plan. I'm going to try to get a couple hours of shut-eye, then I'll take over watch for you."

———◆❈◆———

He woke up in a cold sweat again, choking to catch his breath. That damnable dream. It seemed like every time he went to sleep, he had it. And it was worse than usual since Lou Mancini, his supplier, had threatened him about paying up.

He had dreamt he was in college again, pledging the fraternity. The hazing had been awful—more than anyone should have to put up with. They'd kept the pledge class up for days. They'd forced them to eat insects, worms, live spiders, and, worst of all, cat feces! He could still smell the stench! He could still feel how it gooed between his teeth. He'd finally lost it and yelled, tears streaming down his face, what a bunch of bullshit it was and that he was walking. That's when they'd called him a pansy and had beaten the crap out of him. In his dream he was still on the floor of that damp, musty basement in the frat house, grabbing his nuts, gasping moldy air, and retching up blood and cat shit. And his brother had been at the door, laughing with the others.

His brother. This whole mess was really *his* fault. His brother should have warned him what to expect during hazing. He hadn't tried to save him. He hadn't told the guys to stop. He hadn't watched out for him, which is what older brothers are supposed to do. He'd laughed. And then they'd closed the basement door and walked away.

The pain had been unbearable. He'd been in the hospital for ten days after he'd been found. They'd pumped steroids and morphine in him till he couldn't see straight. His ribs seemed to take months to heal, but that was the least of his worries. The frat brothers had ruptured his testicles. The surgeons had to remove them...and he'd had to live with the pain and humiliation of *that* ever since. *Castrated!* That's why he started drinking so much. To stop the pain. That's why he started doing all those drugs. Anything to get away from the pain and from reality. His brother could still date. His brother could get married and have kids. His brother could keep a job and save money. His brother could do anything, and *did*.

He couldn't do any of that. No more girls, no wife, no steady job, no kids. Just pain, deformity, booze and drugs. That f...ing brother had ruined his life!

Now Lou Mancini was after him to pay up. Lou'd let him slide for a while since he was between jobs again, but now it was payday. Lou was threatening to send his muscle to break his face—the only part of him that was still okay. The only part of him that wasn't damaged.

Yep, it was his damned brother's fault. That's why he'd had to do this. He had to have the money—now. What was $500,000 to him? Nothing. A drop in the bucket.

"Fuck him," he said aloud. "I should have demanded more."

CHAPTER 10

Kate

─────◉─────

Saturday Morning

Dawn finally arrived, the day clear, the temperature cool and the wind brisk. I got out of my car, still feeling clammy after the vision of my parents' accident, and shivered. As I stretched the cramps out of my back and neck, Amy and Carlos pulled up and emerged from their vehicle, grinning.

More coffee, hot this time. I took a cup gratefully and sipped, wishing I'd thought to bring a toothbrush. My teeth felt furry and I'm sure my breath smelled like something had crawled in my mouth and died. I wondered where the nearest port-a-potty was.

Amy and Carlos had checked in with Lieutenant Whitaker after Gomez had called last night, so they were as up-to-date as I. We walked across the street to Wenn Park, being careful not to disturb the scene. I didn't really expect to find anything helpful. But sometimes I can feel some sort of presence if I stand right where the crime took place.

I felt nothing! No fear, nothing threatening. Weird. After looking around for a while, I excused myself and told the others I'd meet them back at the Bryant house. I wandered toward the east end of the park, still feeling nothing disturbing or out of order. "Humph…no trail of breadcrumbs either," I grumbled.

I crossed two streets and stopped at a corner gas station to relieve my bladder and to splash some water on my face. Looking in the mirror, I scared myself! No wonder Carlos and Amy had been grinning when they saw me. I raked my hands through my hair and patted it down the best I could. Unlike Penn Allister, I don't normally care if I have everything in place, but *this* was ridiculous! They should have said something, professional courtesy and all that. I didn't say what I was thinking. My Grandmothers wouldn't have approved.

I returned to the house on Westminster Terrace, promising myself I'd pack some basic necessities in my big black bag after this! I also promised myself to get Amy and Carlos back one of these days!

Whitaker was there when I arrived and asked me to step into the sunroom with him. It wasn't all that warm in the room, but his forehead was dotted with beads of perspiration. "Well, what do you think, Kate?"

I told him about my vision of the man lying in fetal position. I did *not* tell him about my parents—that's too private. We talked about the feelings I'd had or, more appropriately *didn't* have when walking around in the park. "I don't know what to think, Doug. I'm confused right now," I admitted. "I'm not sure what to say. Maybe if I let it ride for a while, I'll come up with something."

"All right, Kate," he replied, sighing. "But I hope you come up with something fast. Tomorrow's Sunday already. Ransom drop is on Tuesday."

Don't remind me! I thought.

"I've got to go with Bryant to the bank before noon, to help him set up the money in case we don't find the child before then. Keep in touch, Kate."

—◆►❈◄◆—

Disheartened, I drove home. My brain felt fuzzy after such a long night. Even after having that cup of coffee, all I wanted to do was crash.

I rummaged around in the refrigerator, looking for something to eat. Nothing sounded good. I munched on a little chunk of cheese that hadn't yet turned green. The milk jug was so old it had swollen up, ready to explode. Gingerly, I took it to the sink and carefully untwisted the lid. It made a hissing sound as gas escaped. *This is disgusting,* I thought, as I poured the gross stuff down the sink. The smell made me gag.

I plunked down at my desk, head in hands. I glanced over at my answering machine. It was totally dark, which reminded me that I'd broken the stupid thing when I'd dropped it last night. I needed to replace the fool thing.

"*Crud!*" I muttered. I grabbed my bag and keys, paused at the closet for my favorite suede jacket, and left to find lunch and a new phone.

I ended up at Lenox Mall. As I was riding down the escalator to the food court, lost in my own thoughts, I heard someone call my name. Turning, I spotted Gloria.

"Hey, girl. What'cha doin?" she called out...loudly.

I almost choked! Glory was "all doodied-up", as my father used to say when describing someone who was outrageously dressed. She wore a grass-green leather *short*-short skirt with a matching bustier. And stiletto heels. Glory teetered precariously a few stairs behind me on the escalator. All eyes were on her. No surprise there!

I got off at the bottom, wishing the floor would swallow me up, but instead waited until she caught up with me. "Hey yourself," I said. "I'm going to grab a sandwich and some coffee. Join me?"

Glory flashed a perfect set of teeth and her eyes glittered as she teased, "I suppose I can eat with you, although you don't look nearly as high-class as me."

*As I...*I thought, but kept my mouth closed. It is a moot point to discuss grammar with someone who wears chartreuse leather.

We looked like a rather unlikely pair as we ate our lunches and chatted. "When do I get to come with you on a case?" asked Glory as she munched.

"One of these days…" I replied, trying not to commit. I had to smile at the thought of her trying to be subtle and inconspicuous in her leather outfit. Somehow it just wouldn't work. However if I ever need someone to create a diversion…

Glory broke into my thoughts and almost knocked over her drink as she grabbed my arm. "Kate," she hissed. "That's him…I think so, anyway!"

"What on *earth* are you talking about?" I asked, completely puzzled.

She got a real sheepish look on her face. "I guess I forgot to tell you…uh…first thing this morning a guy came into the parking garage and asked Sally, the other guard, if he could get into your apartment. She called me, since you weren't home and anyway, we're friends. I told her not to let him go up—you hadn't said anything about any workman coming over.

"Anyway, on my way over here, I stopped by the garage and had a look at the video tape. It was pretty fuzzy, but I looked really close. I could be way off, here, but it sure looks like the guy that just walked past!"

I started to turn around to look, but Glory hissed again, "No! Don't turn around! He just went into "Exercise and Fitness R Us". Oh-my-god! What are we gonna do?!"

My curiosity was piqued, but *Glory* was out of control. She was bouncing in her chair and I was afraid her boobs were going to pop right out!

"Cool it, Gloria," I whispered, leaning forward. "I need a bit more info before I do anything. Did Sally say anything else about him?"

"Lemme think…Yeah. He said his name was Max something-or-other and wanted to go in and paint. You want me to go over and ask him? He's still in the fitness store."

"*You* aren't going to do anything. There's a chance he doesn't know what I look like. Besides, I'm finished eating. I'll go over there and pretend to browse. Maybe they know him. I'll try to figure out something.

"Just stay put and let me handle this. You've been a great help already. Now, tell me what he's got on, so I know which guy I'm after."

I nonchalantly took my tray and emptied my trash. Then I walked very slowly over to the shop and looked at the items in the display window. Pretending to find something interesting, as if I'd even *know* what exercise equipment is, I made my way into the store.

Meanwhile, Glory was still bouncing up and down in her seat, gathering stares from all directions. *You can't make me just* sit *here while* you *have all the fun!* She glanced around at the shops. She needed to do something...but what? She grabbed her tray and shoved it into the hands of a senior citizen who was wiping tables. "Here...take this!

"...please, sir," she added, politely and flashed him a smile. "Police business!"

He didn't notice her smile. His eyes were glued to the bustier.

She dashed, as fast as her stiletto heels would permit, into a card store. "Do y'all have any, like, birthday cameras, you know... for parties?" she asked, breathlessly.

"Uh...we've got these disposable ones..." said the surprised teen behind the register. He ogled her breasts which were threatening to burst out into the open.

"Perfect!" she shouted, grabbed one and tossed some bills at the astonished clerk. "Keep the change," she shouted as she scurried out the door, tushie wiggling.

People cleared out of her way as she raced back to her table in the food court. She sat back down, snatched the wrapper off the camera, and aimed. *I don't have a gun,* she thought, *but this just might be better!*

———◆❈◆———

I was completely unaware of the commotion in the food court and was making my way around the shop, looking at brochures of different brands of equipment, and trying to think of an intelligent question in case a salesperson approached. I wasn't having much luck since besides a little Tae Kwan Do, I know nothing about exercising. My brain was full of *other* questions instead.

Questions like…Who's this 'Max'? Is that his real name? If not, how am I going to find out what it really is? Why had he been trying to get in my apartment? Was he really a painter? Or does he work for someone else? Is he connected to Eddie's kidnapping somehow?

"Oh!" I yelped as I tripped over a salesperson who was kneeling on the floor. He was removing weights from a box and I hadn't even seen him. I landed flat on top of him! How embarrassing is *that*?

I jumped up, checked to make sure I hadn't killed the poor fellow (nope, he was still breathing) and attempted to regain control of myself.

Instantly, every eye was focused on me, including the muscled "Max". *Way to be inconspicuous, Kate,* I admonished myself. Max did a double-take at me and ran.

Mentally kicking myself…again, I looked around helplessly and asked, "Do you guys happen to know that man's name? Uh…" *Think fast,* I told myself.

"…My nephew has seen him at the workout center and um… wants to know if he can…uh…get his autograph. My nephew is just little, so he's into great big, muscle-y guys."

I did a mental eye roll. I've been doing a lot of those recently! *Boy, was that lame.*

But the sales clerk bought my line and answered. "Yeah…He comes in here every once in a while and buys equipment. He's putting together a home gym. The guy works out all the time. Says he's a bouncer or something at some downtown club and needs to stay in shape. His name's Ronnie Walker."

I felt faint. "Thanks," I stammered. "You wouldn't know which club, would you?"

"Nah…it's downtown though, across from that new martini bar."

"Oh. Well, thanks, again," I managed to say brightly as I headed out the door.

Once in the food court again, I collapsed in the chair opposite Glory. "God! That was a disaster! I didn't figure he'd recognize me, but he obviously did. Did you see him take off?"

Glory sat there, calmly, with a huge "cat that ate the canary" grin on her face. Then she raised the camera into my line of vision. "Got 'im!"

"What?" I asked. Then I smiled when it dawned on me what she had done. "You're brilliant, girl!"

We both got up and collected ourselves.

I told Glory, "I got his real name. I'm going to hurry up and buy a phone. Then I'll do some investigating on this Ronnie Walker guy. Maybe he's connected to this new case I'm working on."

"Well, I'm going to drop these pictures off at the one-hour photo lab. I'll catch up with you back at your place before I go to work…okay partner?"

Partner?! Oh my god!

CHAPTER II

Westminster Terrace

———— ✦ ————

Saturday Noon

Emerson Bryant arrived at the house on Westminster Terrace just before noon and joined his brother in the library. It was still nippy outside, so Arlington had started a fire and invited Emerson to sit with him and have coffee.

"I'm running on this stuff," commented Arlington, indicating the cup in front of him. His eyes were bloodshot and his hands shook.

"What have you heard?" Emerson queried, concern in his voice.

"Not a damned thing since last night. I thought they would have called by now. I wonder what's taking them." He sighed and added, "Poor kid. He must be scared half to death. And Penn—she's beside herself."

Emerson sipped his coffee and stared into the fire. Out of the corner of his eye he could see an officer monitoring the phone on the desk.

Unable to sit still any longer, Arlington jumped up and paced the room. "I'm going nuts here!" he shouted, causing both Emerson and the police officer to jump. "I hate this sitting around!"

Moments later, the phone rang. Everyone froze. On the second ring, the officer placed his hand on his receiver and the record button, and then nodded to Arlington, who picked up the cordless phone next to the couch.

"Bryant," he answered, his voice tense. His eyes were squinted half-closed as he concentrated on the voice at the other end. "Tuesday, six p.m. Okay. Where again? ...Which terminal? Okay. How will I get him back? How do I know Eddie's still all right? Let me talk to him...please...But..."

Click. The line went dead. "Shit!" Arlington exclaimed.

"Wait," the officer said. "You kept him on longer this time. Maybe we'll get something. Hang in there Mr. Bryant. You did real good."

Arlington began to pace again, wringing his hands together. As he turned, Penn Allister flew through the door, her eyes wide.

"What?!" she breathed, hovering expectantly.

The officer, an expert in tracing calls reported excitedly, "We've narrowed it down to this quadrant of the city! They're close by. This really helps!" He grabbed his radio and made a call to Lieutenant Whitaker at the station.

"Arlington, what did he say?" Penn Allister asked her husband.

"Um...Half a million...at the airport...Tuesday night...six o'clock. International terminal—F. At the parking garage there. After they count the money, they'll call again and let us know where to get Eddie. He wouldn't let me talk to him. But the guy said he's fine."

"Not till Tuesday?" Penn said, sinking into a chair. "My baby... my poor baby!" and began to sob quietly.

Emerson stood and walked over to the window, placing a comforting hand on Penn Allister's shoulder as he passed. "He's going to be all right, you two. He's a tough little kid, you know. He'll be okay. If you do as they ask, they won't have any reason to hurt him."

CHAPTER 12

Kate's Loft

Saturday Afternoon

I finally got back from Lenox Mall and took the time to set up my new phone system. Instead of taking a nap as I probably should have, the caffeine from lunch kicked in and I puttered around, trying to get a line on this Max/Ronnie fellow, mulling events over in my mind, doing some laundry, watering my plants and paying a couple bills.

As the afternoon wore on, I continued to puzzle over my latest visions—the guy curled up on the floor somewhere and my parents' accident. Why did I see these things? Why were these visions so close together, time-wise? Were the two connected in some way? Did they somehow connect to Eddie Bryant's kidnapping?

Lieutenant Whitaker called in the middle of the afternoon. "Hey, Doug," I answered in my most upbeat tone. *Good thing I'd installed my new phone!*

Whitaker informed me of the second call from the kidnappers. We discussed the arrangements we would need to make with the

Hartsfield Airport officials. It's not too easy to take a half million dollars through security. He said he'd handle it from his end and let me know if I would be needed during the drop—if things got that far. Of course, we were both hoping to find Eddie, safe and sound, long before Tuesday evening.

People at the Bryant home were waiting to hear from the captors again with more details about the drop site. Whitaker also told me the good news—that they'd narrowed down the location of the phone call to the northeast section of Atlanta. We discussed my visions, and this time I mentioned the one about my parents. Whether it was just random or if it fit this case, I still wasn't sure. In passing, I mentioned that someone had tried to get into my loft, using a fake name.

"What?!" Whitaker responded. "When? What name did he use? Describe him. How do you know 'Max' is a fake name?"

He laughed right out loud when I described the scene at Lenox Mall. "I'm hoping to hear from Gloria any minute," I added. "She's going to bring the developed pictures when she goes on duty this afternoon."

"Good work. So…Ronnie Walker is his real name…Do you want to access our files to see if you can find out any more information on this guy? If you need to, I'll leave clearance at the front desk. We've got a new person on tonight—might not let you in if you're not a uniformed officer."

We disconnected just as my doorbell rang. It was Glory. "Hey, partner," she started. I did another mental eye roll. "Are we good, or what? I just saw Sally in the garage, showed her my *excellent* photos of this hunk and she ID'd him. Said he was Max, the painter. I didn't tell her his *real* name since this is an official police investigation."

"You did real well, Glory. Thanks. Wish you could hang out with me. We'd try to get some more info on Walker, but I know you have to go to work. I guess I'll try on my own."

"Yeah…Sally's waiting for me to get back downstairs—she's got a date tonight. "Working Saturday night just sucks, you know… really puts a crimp in my style!

And…I have to be back on duty again tomorrow at noon! I wonder who sets up these schedules…"

Gloria continued to grumble as she tossed the pictures on my desk and headed back to the elevator. I felt kind of sorry for her—just like I was feeling sorry for myself. As I think I mentioned earlier, my Saturday night dates were non-existent, too.

I was considering drowning my sorrows in some type of alcohol—or perhaps chocolate—when my phone rang again. It was my brother David, who invited me to the old home place for dinner. He knows what kind of cook I am and, of course, I gratefully accepted, since *I* know what kind of cook I am, too!

I'd been so busy lately that I hadn't seen him, his wife Sarah, or Grandma Jeffers in quite some time. Anyway, a change of scenery might be very helpful—get me out of my Saturday night blues, if nothing else. I told him I'd be there close to six.

I cleaned myself up a little and then headed over to the station to do some snooping on Ronnie Walker before driving up to Buckhead.

CHAPTER 13

Ronnie

⚫

Saturday Afternoon

Ronnie pulled close to the entrance of Kate Jeffers' parking garage. He'd done some more homework. He knew her car. He was still shaken from his close call at Lenox Mall. Hopefully her presence was just coincidental and she had no idea who he was. Or maybe she was still busy extricating herself from that embarrassing situation in the fitness store when he'd run out of there. Maybe she'd taken no notice of him at all. He chided himself—he was getting paranoid.

He watched as she drove in and spoke to the security guard. It was the same one that had been on duty earlier and he didn't want to encounter her again.

Even if someone else had been on duty he wouldn't risk going upstairs with Jeffers being home—no way! So he merely watched as Jeffers got into the elevator.

Her place sounded like something! Ronnie'd done some checking on that, too. The girl lived on the top floor of the building. It had been an office or a storage room a long time ago and then some reclaim-the-city group had bought the building and made condos and what-have-you out of the different spaces.

Ronnie grabbed his laptop and typed in some new information. He chuckled. It's amazing what you can get on a person via the internet! He checked out Kate Jeffers' bank accounts. *Where the hell'd she come up with this kind of money?* he asked himself. *She on the take?* He continued to type. A few seconds later he came up with her family information. Her parents had been killed in an accident when she'd been twelve. Raised by grandparents after that. Two siblings, David, now age twenty-three and Emily, twenty-one.

He glanced up from his work, thinking. He wondered why Lou had gotten so upset when he'd heard that name. Had their paths crossed before? Did she know something about him?

In order to find out what, if anything, she knew about his boss or about this kidnapping, he'd have to get inside her apartment. His first attempt sure hadn't worked! He needed a plan...

He still liked the painter idea—maybe he could just tweak it a little.

As he watched, another guard came along and talked to Sally. This *new* one was H-O-T! She disappeared into the elevator and Ronnie got bored again.

Then here she came again. This time the good-looking one took over and the one called Sally left.

"Man—what a goooood-looking chic!" Ronnie exclaimed right out loud. "Maybe I'll have better luck with this one—more ways than one!" And he began to daydream some *very* x-rated thoughts.

Ronnie continued his musings and formulated a couple of plans as the afternoon drifted on.

Around five his attention was back on the parking garage. He fired up his engine when he saw Kate Jeffers emerge from the elevator. She got into her car, exited the garage, and headed east. He followed.

Ronnie parked across from the Monroe Street Police Station and watched as Kate hurried through the doors.

She was inside for almost an hour, and then was on the move again. This time she headed north on Monroe to Piedmont.

Ronnie lay back in traffic as Jeffers took Piedmont to Pharr Road and turned west. He continued until she pulled up to some huge iron gates at an estate in Buckhead.

He watched as she said something into the speaker box. The gates swung open and Jeffers drove in.

Ronnie parked, hidden by the roadside shrubbery.

He hoisted his briefcase onto his lap, got out his laptop, and began typing again. He needed to find out about this place and more about Kate Jeffers before it was too dark to see.

CHAPTER 14

Kate at the Buckhead Estate

Saturday Evening

Sarah, David's wife of about a year, met me at the door. "You're showing!" I exclaimed and had a hard time figuring out how to give her a hug without flattening the baby-bulge. I navigated my way around her and hugged her from the side. Sarah's a great girl, petite, dark-haired, very good for Dave. This was their first pregnancy and she looked like it agreed with her. I could hear my biological clock ticking loudly in the background. Funny…it seemed to get louder as I stepped inside. Oops! Just the grandfather clock in the entry hall. *Silly me.*

It turned out that Grandma Jeffers, who'd moved into the gate house on the estate after Dave and Sarah were married, was out with her cronies. So it was just us "young people" as she refers to us.

Our sister, Emily, had a date—after all, it *was* Saturday night!—so couldn't join us either.

We gathered in the kitchen, where Dave opened my proffered bottle of cabernet and poured two glasses (Sarah had water). He was working on dinner, a divine Italian soup with sausages, tomatoes, peppers and zucchini. According to him, any time you start with olive oil, garlic, and onions, you can't go wrong. I have to agree.

The kitchen smelled great: a mixture of Dave's soup and the yeast from Sarah's homemade herb bread, still rising on the counter. *Maybe I can talk* them *into giving me cooking lessons.*

We talked, drank, and laughed, catching up on news while the soup simmered. After Sarah punched down the dough, she made individual loaves and let them rise again. When the bread was in the oven I set the table in the kitchen.

When Grandma was out, we had casual meals as opposed to when she joined us. At those times we "dressed" for dinner and always ate in the dining room. We commented about feeling guilty, sinful and enjoyed every minute.

We talked about the baby's room. They've decided to paint the room a cheerful spring yellow since they don't know the baby's gender. They aren't into the pink and blue scene anyway, thank goodness!

Conversation turned to names for the little one and we came up with some good suggestions.

I asked about Emily, our sister. I haven't talked with her for weeks! She is on my 'to-do' list, but I really want to have a big block of time to spend with her. I feel like we've drifted apart in the past three years since she's been away at school. Even though she's still in Atlanta at the Art Institute, we hardly ever see her. And lately I've been getting some weird vibes concerning her. I need to move Emily up to top priority.

Sarah said Emily was dating a new fellow—a real nice guy. I felt out of the loop again—both with my family and with the dating scene. Dave added that Emily's classes at the Institute are going very well and it appears she has a lot of talent. I wasn't surprised by that—she's always been the creative one. I certainly didn't get any of those genes!

Dinner was delicious. I sopped up the juices of my soup with the last crust of bread. Good thing Grandma wasn't there. She would have reminded me to be more lady-like. At least I didn't lick the bowl!

Dave then brought out some pears and stilton cheese for dessert.

Sarah is at the stage of pregnancy where she tires easily, so she excused herself and headed for bed.

I declined an after dinner port and decided I'd head home after helping Dave with the dishes.

I didn't make it right away.

CHAPTER 15

Kate

Saturday, After Dinner

After I left Sarah and Dave's house, I headed south on Peachtree Road, back toward Midtown and my loft. Man, was I tired. The only thing that sounded good was to maybe soak in a hot tub and to put my little self to bed.

As I stopped at the light at Pharr Road, I happened to notice a car behind me. I hadn't been paying attention and wondered how long it had been there. On green, I started forward and switched lanes once I was out of the intersection. So did the car behind me. I sped up a little. So did it. I tried slowing. Same. "Crap!" I said out loud. "Is this just some asshole that thinks he's cute or does this have something to do with the case?"

I squinted in the reflection of the headlights, but couldn't make out the make of the vehicle or see who was driving. Of course in Georgia there isn't a front license plate, so forget trying to get *that*. And, when I'd grabbed my keys—which seemed like weeks ago—I'd forgotten my cell phone. I could picture it, battery fully charged, sitting on my desk. Great!

The car started to edge around me and was coming up on my left when we got to West Wesley. I acted like I was going straight, and then, at the last second, chucked a right onto West Wesley. There is a little side road off to the left that hooks back onto Peachtree (if I could remember where it was). I heard tires squealing and horns blasting. *Jesus Maria!* Whoever was following me had made a U-turn right on the main road and was coming after me! I saw the sign for the side street and made a quick left. Instantly, I pulled into a driveway, killed the engine and the lights, and lay down across the center console. The gear shift dug into my ribs, my breathing was labored and I was sweating like crazy.

Headlights flashed past the rear of my car and disappeared down the street. Ha! They missed me! Drove right past! *Am I cool, or what?* I congratulated myself.

I wasn't feeling so cool. As a matter of fact, I felt like throwing up. But hey, I was trained for this kind of stuff, right? So, not to worry. I just didn't think I could go home right away. For one thing, whoever was following me might know where I live and, if whoever it was happened to be cute, he could probably sweet-talk his way past Glory. This kind of thing had happened before, and although the management had spoken to her about it, I wasn't convinced their pleas were going to be heeded. If a guy had big pectorals under a tight t-shirt, Glory turned to mush. And if his biceps were…well you get the idea.

Besides, my nerves were shot. Where to go, where to go? Oh, yeah, I know…

CHAPTER 16

Papa's Lounge

———— ● ————

Late Saturday Night

I ended up at Papa's. There are twelve bars within walking distance of my loft, but this one is my favorite. Perhaps because of the bartender/owner, Thomas Papadopoulos. "Papa" has been in (and out) of my life, and my heart, for years, ever since high school. I adore him! He's so cute and so sweet and so hot and, most importantly, doesn't seem to realize it.

When I say cute, I mean from the neck down. He's got great eyes and gorgeous teeth, but his nose is a little crooked. As I recall, he said it got broken in a wrestling match when he was in Middle School. He also said it'd been worth it since he'd pinned the other guy in four seconds after they'd cleaned up the blood! When you look at the whole structure, his face can be considered "interesting" rather than handsome. Maybe that's why he's so unassuming. Good thing I like "interesting".

As you probably guessed from his last name, he's Greek and that's why we're not an item—I'm not. *I* don't have a problem with it, but his family automatically assumes he'll marry a girl from the Greek community. *Well, damn.*

At any rate, I *needed* to see Papa. Needed to look into those dark eyes that can see to my very soul. Have you ever known someone who makes your heart flutter, your stomach clench and your knees go weak just by looking at you? That's Papa. Then, if he happens to wink…well, never mind. I'm getting turned on just thinking about it.

I walked into the bar and checked out the scene…but he wasn't there! *Oh, man!* My stomach fell to the bottom of my shoes. Instant depression! It's ridiculous that anyone can have this kind of effect on me and it makes me furious. I dragged myself over to the bar and climbed on a stool. I know better than to drink when I am in this condition. I was tired, frustrated because I didn't understand my recent visions, a nervous wreck from almost getting run down, and PO'd because Papa wasn't standing at the bar to greet me. I should have gone home. I didn't.

Demetri, the other bar hand, reached over and put a comforting hand on my shoulder. "Hey there, Kate. You look beat. What can I get for you?" Then he whispered, in keeping with his role as my conspirator, "Papa had to leave about fifteen minutes ago. Sorry."

I avoided the Ouzo, having almost killed myself with it a couple of years ago when I was on an "I miss Papa" jag. Instead I ordered some single malt scotch, and sat there sipping the glorious, smooth liquid sliding down my throat. I was still feeling very sorry for myself.

Questions such as "Who was just chasing me?", "Why couldn't I have been born Greek?", "What did those visions mean?" and "Why am I so stupid that I can't figure out this kidnapping thing?" kept running through my mind. Perhaps another scotch would clear my head. *Oh, brother!* That's the kind of thinking that always leads to trouble.

I downed the rest of my drink and Demetri came back. "No thanks, Sweetie," I said when he offered another shot. "No more. You know will happen if I don't leave now." I smiled rather wistfully at him, asked him to give Papa my regards, paid (big tip, as always), and slouched my sorry tail home.

Once there, I mentally kicked myself for my behavior and fixed myself a mug of decaf tea. I smiled. My Grandma Jeffers would have a fit if she could see me now.

"Tea—in a MUG," she would gasp, putting her hand on her chest to help catch her breath. "How gauche! Where are your teacups, Kate?"

It was way too late to call her, so I grabbed a sweatshirt and headed for my patio. I needed to think, process and get my act together.

The night was clear and a bit nippy, even for October. There wasn't much breeze up here on the roof, and I could make out a few stars, although the city lights tend to obscure them.

Just sitting out here, smelling the earth in the pots and beds, breathing the fresh air, contemplating the vastness of the universe, always seems to calm me down. Helps me get a perspective on things. Tonight was no different.

The air smelled musty, like autumn leaves. I allowed my thoughts to wander. I've never minded fall in Atlanta. The days are pretty and not as hot as in the summer. The coming of winter isn't a downer like it is up north, since the winters are mild and by February, the flowers are blooming again. Of course I've always lived in Atlanta, so am biased, I suppose.

I tried to "think" myself into an eight-year-old's position, placing him not here, in my rooftop garden, but in the park, playing on the jungle gym.

Friday's weather had been nice, even though the wind had begun to blow and the temperature had dropped a few degrees by the time he'd been kidnapped.

Eddie knew he had to be home for dinner, but wanted to go hang out in the park for a while. He'd have been able to see anyone who would have approached. No one could have just taken him. He'd have yelled or something. Yep—it *has* to be an inside job.

Whom did he know that would have been able to convince him to go with them? That was going to have to be my approach.

I moved on, analyzing my visions. Perhaps they didn't have anything to do with Eddie at all. Maybe they had something to do with an entirely different occurrence. But that usually doesn't happen to me. Something about whatever case I am working on always seems to trigger a vision. What, then, would some older male lying in fetal position have to do with Eddie? I just couldn't come up with it. Frustrating!

The ringing of my phone brought me back to the present. I hurried inside and my heart did a whomp-whomp as I saw the caller I.D.

Papa! I snatched up the receiver, "Hi!" I squeaked. Quickly, I cleared my throat. "Hi," I said in a more normal tone. I was aiming for "sexy", but didn't quite make it.

That voice on the other end...it was enough to give a girl goosebumps! "Sorry I missed you. Demetri said you'd been in and looked like shit."

Thanks a heap, Demetri! I thought to myself. Aloud, I said, "I'm going to ask him to return my tip next time I see him."

"Not to worry, you could never look that bad." (He hadn't seen me in the morning lately.) "Work getting to you?"

"Yeah," and *the fact I hadn't had sex, good or bad, for an embarrassingly long time,* I added silently.

"Unfortunately, I can't get away tonight," he said. (My throat felt all clogged up and I wondered how he felt about phone sex.) "What's up? Are you okay?"

Oh baby, if you only knew! "Thanks, I'm doing all right now, Papa. It was sweet of you to call—you didn't have to."

"Demetri was pushing it. Not that I didn't *want* to, he just kept saying how crappy you looked."

That did it! "I'm going to have to kill him!"

Laughter from the other end.

"I'm just frustrated about this new case and really tired. I'm headed to bed. Maybe that will help."

"Mmm...alone?"

"Of course...I mean...Yes." *Way to go, stupid. Just flat out* advertise *that you're not going out with anyone!* "A good night's sleep is what I need."

"Oh...All right, then. But let's get together soon, okay? I miss seeing you."

That sexy accent of his gets me every time. "Okay. I'll be in touch."

And I'm supposed to fall asleep after *that*!? I plunked myself in bed and stared at the ceiling for a *long* while.

CHAPTER 17

Ronnie

———— ● ————

Late Saturday Night

"Hell's fire!" he burst out. "Where'd she go?" Ronnie was sitting at the stop sign at the end of Rivers Road, a street that intersects Peachtree after a couple of turns. "She was right in front of me…how'd she spot me? How'd she just disappear? Lou's not going to like this!"

He looked all around, totally confused. "Son of a…," he muttered, and pulled back onto the main drag.

His aim was to scare her off the case or at least make her very nervous. He wasn't trying to get her (or himself) killed. Although Lou'd probably like *that*. That U-turn stunt he'd pulled on Peachtree a few minutes earlier was really stupid! His heart was still hammering in his rib cage.

Ronnie decided he'd go back to the Jeffers' place and wait. It was late and she *had* to come home sometime.

He parked across from the entrance to Jeffers' building's parking garage and willed his breathing back to normal. The good-looking security guard was still on duty. *Man, she must not have any kind of life! Seems as though she works 24/7.*

In his mind, he plotted a way to get to know her better...*and* how to talk his way into Jeffers' apartment.

A while later he noticed a woman walking, well, weaving a little, towards him. It was Jeffers!

What the...? Where've you been, lady? Ronnie silently asked. "And what did you do with your car?" he wondered aloud.

Kate Jeffers entered the garage, gestured wildly while speaking to the guard and then made her way to the elevators.

"Huh..." muttered Ronnie as he fired up the Chevy. "Guess I'll tour the neighborhood. Maybe I'll find her car...or somewhere to hang out for a while before I have to face Lou."

CHAPTER 18

Kate

◉

Sunday Morning

I awoke around nine, a bit befuddled. Not that that is anything new, but there were so many things whirling around in my head. Maybe it was just the scotch, but then again, maybe not.

First of all, Papa was still on my mind. As I said, so what's new?

Secondly, I wondered about the car that had followed me from David's. Why was it following me? Who'd been driving? Did this mean I was onto something? If so, what?! Grr...

I staggered from my bed, thinking that if Rob Abrams, my architect, and I had been smart when we were designing this place, we would have put in an intravenous line from the coffee maker to my bedroom!

Where'd I leave my car? Oh, boy...

Once downstairs, coffee in hand, I sat at my desk and allowed myself to mull over the recent events. As I took notes, I pinned them up on my office cupboard doors.

Eddie Bryant gets kidnapped Friday night.

Later that night, I had a vision about a guy lying on the floor somewhere.

Then I had that recurring one about my parents' accident.

Saturday morning Glory tells me some guy's been trying to get in my apartment.

Next we see him at the mall. He spooks and takes off.

Meanwhile, the kidnappers call again. Ransom is due Tuesday.

Sally I D's the picture of Ronnie Walker, the guy we saw at the mall. The same guy who was trying to get in my loft.

Then I get followed last night after leaving Dave and Sarah's. Same guy? Too bad I didn't get to see his car clearly!

Hmmm…How does this all fit? Where do I need to go from here? I studied all my notes and rearranged a few.

Ronnie Walker…probably small-time or Lieutenant Whitaker would have heard of him. I wondered who he worked for. I was going to start there…some background on this guy.

Thank goodness Rob had had the presence of mind to line the inside of my office doors with corkboard. Being able to rearrange my notes was a life saver!

As if thinking about someone makes them call, the phone rang. It was Rob Abrams, wanting to meet for lunch. I agreed and headed for the shower, secretly wishing it had been Papa who had phoned. I told my evil self to *go away* and washed my hair.

CHAPTER 19

Lou

———————— ● ————————

Sunday Morning

Lou Mancini had slept on the sofa in his office above the club.
Prosciutto's had done a booming business Saturday night,
per usual. Lou had listened to the sounds of the bar crowd as
he'd drifted off. He chided himself about being so attached to his
business, telling himself that he really needed a good night's sleep
in an actual bed—not on a couch. As he rubbed his balding head
and scratched his paunch, his phone rang. He hobbled stiffly over
to his desk and saw Ronnie's number on the caller I.D.

"Hey, kid," he answered.

"Lou. I followed Jeffers again last night. I lost her for a while,
but she turned up again. I got a lot of info on her and I've come
up with a plan to get into her place and have a little look around—
probably today. When I'm finished, I'll report back to you."

"All right, but not till later," Lou replied. "I'm going to have to
get out of here for a little while. I'm stir-crazy."

"What? Did you spend the night there again? Man, you *do* need to get a life," answered Ronnie, jokingly. "You spend way too much time there.

"When and where do you want to meet?" he added in a serious tone when Lou made it clear he wasn't in a jovial mood.

Lou answered, "Why don't you come here tonight? Around eight or nine. That will leave me some time to get a few things done this afternoon."

"You got it," and Ronnie hung up. He headed home for some shut-eye before carrying out his plan.

CHAPTER 20

Kate and Rob

———— ◈ ————

Lunch, Sunday

R ob picked me up in the parking garage just after noon on Sunday. He said he'd gotten pretty well caught up with his current project and could "spare me some time". I didn't like the way he put it, but hey, I was hungry, and heaven knew I wasn't going to cook anything.

I sketched a wave to Glory and told her we'd talk when I got back. I hopped in Rob's Jag and we roared down the street. He headed over 10th Street to Virginia Highlands where we stopped at a fabulous seafood and oyster bar.

The food was great; the conversation lacking. I asked him about the house he was designing, but he didn't volunteer much information. It was as though his mind was elsewhere.

He dutifully inquired about my latest case, but wasn't really paying attention when I briefed him on the events that weren't too confidential. I guess when we were finished with my loft we ceased having much in common.

In spite of the food and atmosphere, lunch was pretty depressing. All those delicious oysters, wasted.

On the way out of the restaurant, Rob must have had a change of heart. He asked me if I wanted to drive past his new building site. "We're pretty close. It's just a couple blocks east of here." He must have been feeling guilty for being so inattentive as we ate.

We started east and BAM, a vision hit.

My loft! I could see someone rummaging through my desk! There isn't anything anyone would want, just paper clips, and so forth, but what the *hell* was someone doing in my loft?!

"Rob, I'm sorry, but I've got to get back. NOW!"

"Don't worry," he replied, oblivious to the hysteria in my voice. "This won't take very long."

God, I *hate* it when people doesn't listen to me! I didn't want to sound panicky, but that's how I felt. He doesn't know about my visions and I really didn't want to go there, but I needed to get home!

"Uh..." I started. "I'm going to be sick!"

Now is that quick thinking, or not? I made a gagging noise and slapped both hands over my mouth.

Brakes squealed! I assume they were Rob's, but who knows? He swerved to the curb as cars behind us skittered all over the street, horns blaring. I gave the car door a shove and tumbled out onto the sidewalk.

I glanced over my shoulder as I stood up and could have sworn that someone in a passing car stuck up one digit on his right hand as he flashed by. *Jeeze. Some people!*

I made noises like I was up-chucking (behind the car where Rob couldn't see) and then wiped my mouth on my hand as I stood and knew I was visible in his rearview mirror.

I can be a good actress in a crisis situation!

I *still* can't believe what happened next. He LOCKED the freaking doors! My window came down about two inches and he leaned across and said, "Sorry, but I've got to get back to work."

He pushed a twenty through the little slit in the window and added, "Take a cab."

My eyes got big and my mouth dropped open. "Take a *cab*? You...you...slime-bucket!" I screeched. "You piece of manuna! You..." And I added a few other terms that the grandmothers would disapprove of.

He shoved the Jag into gear and peeled off down the street.

Can you believe it? Actually, I *do* believe it. He *loves* that car! God forbid someone should urp in it.

Well, in his wake, the twenty floated to the curb. Not that I'm mercenary or anything, but I picked it up. Money's money and his is as green as the next guy's.

I crossed the street so I was headed toward home, and hailed a cab.

◆─◆

Glory's eyes popped as I got out of the taxi and paid the guy. "I thought...," she began.

"Don't even ask!" I replied.

"Wait! What happened? Did you guys break up? I've always thought he was no good for you. I want details...Tell me!"

Her boobs were doing the bouncing thing again. *They* get more exercise than *I* do!

"Why didn't Abrams bring you home?" she called out as I ran to the elevator and pressed the button.

"Tell you later...I think I've got a problem upstairs." The elevator doors closed as I watched a puzzled look cross her face.

On the way up in the elevator, I remembered my car sitting in Papa's parking lot. Something else I had to deal with!

I entered the loft cautiously. Something didn't feel right. I looked around and didn't notice anything out of place. In the vision, someone had been at my desk, but things looked normal.

I grabbed a latex glove from the box I keep on the corner of the desk (yes, I *do* keep a box handy) and opened the drawers. Nothing seemed out of place.

Then I swiveled the chair around and opened the closet doors. One drawer was slightly open.

I'm anal about some things. I'd *never* close the closet doors without making certain all the drawers were shut.

My stomach clenched and I really *did* feel like I was going to get sick when I pulled open the drawer. It was trashed! Files were all jumbled up. Papers were strewn every direction.

It would take *weeks* to get everything sorted and back in place!

"Oh, crap!" I yelled and, still gloved, picked up the phone to call Lieutenant Whitaker.

CHAPTER 21

Ronnie and Glory

———————— ● ————————

Sunday Noon

As soon as the Jeffers broad left with the guy in the Jag, Ronnie made his move. Ronnie swaggered up to Glory's desk in the parking garage. He was going to try to talk his way in again, so he dressed for the part, wearing white painter's pants and a skin-tight white t-shirt, both slightly smeared with paint. He carried a small pail and had a couple brushes in his pocket. He thought maybe he'd have better luck with this guard than with the other one who'd been here on Friday. She is kinda cute, even up close; he thought and decided to turn on the charm. "Hello there…" he murmured in his sexiest baritone. He stared at the name tag on her chest. "So…you're Gloria?"

Glory licked her lips and gave him her best smile. *What angel dropped you here, cutie?* Any thoughts about being wary went right out of her head. *This guy is hot!* She shook her head, trying to collect herself. *You lost one job falling for a guy like this,* she argued with herself. *Come on, woman, don't you be lettin' your hormones carry you away again!*

"Good afternoon. How may I help you?" she asked politely, although she continued to think illicit thoughts. She had to grab the corners of her desk to keep from toppling over.

Doggies, thought Ronnie. *I know this woman's soft spots.* He smiled inwardly, congratulating himself.

He had looked up more facts about Kate Jeffers. She was seeing an architect named Robinson Abrams. He was the same guy who'd redone the penthouse loft for her. And they were out to lunch right now.

"I'm Max," he lied in such a smooth voice that Glory completely forgot that that wasn't his real name. "Mr. Abrams asked me to go up to Ms. Jeffers' loft and touch up a couple places." He lifted the pail, indicating the paint.

"Well, sir, Ms. Jeffers isn't in right now...Wait a minute... Max...you were here the other day, weren't you?"

"Yes, I was and spoke to the other guard, but it was an inconvenient time. Mr. Abrams said to come back today." Ronnie continued in soothing tones, "Mr. Abrams said I could get the key from you and do the painting while he and Ms. Jeffers were at lunch. That way most of the smell will be gone by the time they got back."

That does *make sense,* thought Glory. *He must have talked to Abrams if he knows they're out to lunch. I wonder why they didn't tell me.*

"When I'm finished, maybe you and I could get something to eat. How's that sound? What time do you get off?"

I'm gettin' off right now, sugar, I hate to be tellin' you, she thought and white-knuckled the corners of her desk even harder than before. "I'm here till 7:30 tonight. I only get a little while for lunch and I brought it with me," replied Glory. She was pleased with herself for keeping her act together in the presence of this fine hunk of man.

"Oh, that's too bad," answered Ronnie. He was a little surprised that he actually felt disappointed that she wasn't available. "Now, what about the key? You suppose you could let me have it?"

Baby, that's not all I could let you have...Oh girl...stop thinkin' like this! "I guess it would be all right, since Mr. Abrams told you.

Here you go," she said, handing over Kate's spare key. "Just take that elevator right over there and press '9'. That'll take you right up to the top floor."

"Great. Thanks a lot. I won't be too long and I'll check back in with you before I leave, okay?" Ronnie then walked slowly toward the bank of elevators, allowing Glory a gooood view of his backside.

Gloria sighed and rested her chin on her hands, admiring the view.

Ronnie chuckled as the elevator climbed to the top of the building.

The elevator opened right opposite Jeffers' door. Ronnie donned latex gloves, inserted the key, and let himself in. Once inside the loft, he wasted no time. He went directly to Kate's desk and looked through the drawers. Damn! Nothing here. Next, Ronnie turned to the bi-fold paneled doors behind her desk. *Nice wood. Man, they spared no expense in this place. I wonder if she's got any jewelry I could hock? Too bad I didn't carry a bigger paint can. Well, I can always come back.*

In the huge closet, Ronnie found several drawers full of files. He pawed through them, looking for the one he wanted. "Bingo! Got it," he said.

He left the other files in a heap in the drawer, folded the one he needed, and opened his can of "paint". He stuffed the contents into the paint can and sealed it up again. Then he walked to the kitchen and rinsed one of his brushes. *Can't walk out of here with a dry brush*, he thought. *This Gloria's hot stuff, that's for sure, and who knows—maybe she's smart, too. I gotta be careful.*

Ronnie took a quick survey of the place, appreciating the surroundings, before locking the door, stuffing his gloves in a pocket and descending in the elevator.

He gave Gloria a wide grin as he handed back Jeffers' key. "All finished," he said. "Thanks for your help. Smell should be gone within the hour."

"Mmmm," replied Gloria. "No problem."

"Sorry you're not off work soon. Maybe some other time...?"

"Uh-huh," she murmured dreamily.

Ronnie drove away and pulled into a shady parking space a couple blocks from Kate's building. He wanted to inspect the contents of the file and have everything straight in his mind before his meeting with Lou later on.

Glory sat at the security desk, daydreaming about the man who'd just left. Suddenly, she snapped upright. "Jesus H!" she screeched. "I just let that guy into Kate's place…that Max or Ronnie or whatever his name is. Oh, my god! What have I done? Kate is gonna to *kill* me!"

She was so distraught that she paid no attention to anything until she saw Kate emerge from a taxi. But she'd *left* in Abram's car. Glory was completely confused. "What happened? Did you guys have a fight? Tell me!"

But Kate mumbled something about having a problem and hurried into the elevator.

Glory decided to wait a few minutes before calling Kate to let her know the terrible mistake she'd made.

CHAPTER 22

Kate's Loft

●

Sunday Afternoon

C arlos and Amy stopped by less than ten minutes after Whitaker called them. "You didn't touch anything, did you?" Amy asked.

"I handled the door knob. But everything else I touched with gloves." *I am a cop, you know,* I thought testily. "I walked around the rest of the place. Nothing looks out of place—just the one drawer."

"Any idea what they were after?"

"No. Obviously a file, but I can't tell which, if any, are missing!"

"We'll have the finger printers in this afternoon. Are your case files in that drawer?" Carlos asked.

"Yeah. I've even got a few notes I've taken on the Bryant case, but if you look right here," I said, pointing to the corkboard, "it looks like all *those* are intact."

"We'll call the precinct again and tell them there could be a security breech. That'll hurry the guys up. Once they're finished, have a look through and let Whitaker know what's missing."

"Okay. I'm on my way over there anyway. I need to talk to Doug about a few things. Thanks, you two."

"Any more visions about the little boy?" Amy asked on their way out.

"Nothing I can make any sense of..." and I sighed, feeling totally depressed.

"Don't worry," Carlos said kindly. "We'll get to the bottom of all this soon."

The finger print team arrived soon after Amy and Carlos had left. I stood in the middle of the living room, literally pulling out my hair and getting antsy about going through my files to see what was missing. The printers were careful, but no matter what they do, there's nasty, gray smudgy fingerprint powder everywhere. I'm not a neat-freak, but this was awful. I imagined how long it would take for me to wipe down the place when they were through. I really didn't want to waste the time.

My phone rang, startling everyone. It was Whitaker. "How soon will you be here?" he asked without preamble.

"Soon...I'm just walking out the door..."

One of the finger printers rolled his eyes at me. "The boss?" he asked.

"Hmm."

"Well, look. If he's in that big a hurry, go on over. It'll take us a while here—maybe another hour. You'll be back, won't you? We'll save any questions we have for you until then."

The phone rang again. This time it was Glory. "You seem to be having a lot of company up there this afternoon. Uh...when you came in earlier, there was something I forgot to tell you."

"I'm sorry, Glory. I just can't talk right now. The place was broken into and I've got the finger printers here, and Whitaker's having a fit 'cause I'm not over there yet." I let my voice trail off. What else could go wrong today?

"That's what I needed to talk to you about." Her voice was practically a whisper.

"I'll be right down," I said as I closed my eyes and slowly shook my head. I could feel a headache coming on.

CHAPTER 23

Kate & Whitaker

———————⬤———————

Sunday Afternoon

The first thing I did (after listening to Glory's confession) was trudge over to Papa's lot to retrieve my car. Then I had one other quick errand to run before seeing Whitaker.

Upon my return to the Monroe Street Station, I stuck my head into Doug's office. He was "thinking" with his feet propped up on his desk and his eyes closed.

"Lieutenant, I'm here. I'll be right in. We may have gotten a break in the Eddie Bryant case."

His feet clunked to the floor as he sat upright, his eyes wide open and piercing, showing his sharp intelligence.

I shed my jacket and threw it onto a chair in the hall, talking the whole time. "I just talked to Gloria. She let Ronnie Walker, a.k.a. Max the painter, into my place.

"You *know* how she is…he got her all hot and bothered, and she lost her head. He used the fake name and she didn't catch it. She didn't even remember it was *Sunday* until he was long gone…and heaven knows no workman is going to work on Sunday!

"At least we know who it is," I continued. "After I talked to her, I ran back up to the loft. I was pretty sure which file was going to be missing…and, sure enough, that's the one that is gone. I told the finger printers what was going on, but they wanted to continue anyway."

"Talk to me," Whitaker replied while secretly thinking, *she's so funny when she's on a rip like this. She gets so wound up.*

"I'm not sure where to begin, lieutenant. There's a lot that happened years ago, both to my family and to the Bryants, and I think there's a connection somehow. But without my file…"

I paused, looking at Whitaker. He seemed distracted. "You okay?"

Whitaker leaned back in his seat, trying not to take in the view. *Here she is…pacing this tiny office's floor, dragging her fingers through that unruly mop of hers…flailing her hands…*

He stopped his musings and realized she'd asked him a question. "What? Oh, yes. Go on, I'm listening,"

"First off, here are the pictures of this guy named Ronnie Walker. He's the one who wanted to get into my loft early yesterday morning…and succeeded this afternoon. Recognize him?"

Whitaker looked at the photo and shook his head.

"When I was scouting around at the mall, a salesman in the fitness store said Walker works at a club downtown. He didn't remember the name of the place, but he gave me the general location and said it was run by a guy who's pretty unscrupulous.

I swung past there on my way over here this afternoon, and I think he's talking about Prosciutto's. I punched that into my laptop and came up with the owner's name. Lou Mancini."

"Ah-ha!" Whitaker said, leaning forward and resting his elbows on the desk. "I *have* heard of *him*. He's pretty well known in the drug world. Been on the scene for years…we just can't catch him at anything. And you think Walker works for him?"

"Yes, I'm pretty certain of it. But I'd like to do some more research in the newspaper archives. I think I can tie Mancini to the Bryants. And I need to talk to another contact who knows the

Bryant family's history better than I. (I meant my Grandmother Jeffers, but he didn't need to know that.)

"If I remember correctly, Emerson had some trouble years ago..." I let that comment die since I couldn't remember the details.

"Also," I continued, "the missing file deals with my parents' accident, thirteen years ago. I never really accepted the fact that it was an accident. Something told me that it was deliberate—that they were murdered."

"One of your visions?" I nodded, swallowed the lump in my throat, took a deep breath and said, "I went through that file not too long ago and I swear I remember seeing the name "Mancini" in there somewhere. But here's the deal! When Walker got into my apartment today, *that's* the only file he took! The one containing my parent's accident *and* containing Mancini's name."

I could feel my excitement mount. "Let me go do some checking. If I can tie this with the Bryants..."

"If this is tied in to the Bryant kidnapping, we're going to need to break this open soon. We only have until Tuesday evening.

"Kate," Whitaker added, "be careful. I don't know what else you had in that file, but if you suspect you're in danger, get one of our people to stick with you. You're a civilian now, don't forget. I can't have you in harm's way."

I ignored his warning and headed out.

I stopped home before going to the library archives.

The finger printer started his prattle the second I entered my loft. "The perp, and you think it's this Ron Walker fellow, must've been wearing gloves. The only prints in the place are yours.

"Hey, don't you ever have company?" he joked.

I sighed and felt my shoulders slump. Did another mental eye roll. *Don't remind me,* I thought.

"Anyway, we cross-checked them with the ones on file at the station.

"These computer programs are so cool..."

Geek, I thought. *Nerd. Get out of here and take your damn graphite powder with you!*

The guy was still rambling "…relay the info to Whitaker. Sorry we had to make such a mess. Have fun cleaning up." He smiled as they packed their bags and left.

After I let them out, I bolted the door and was hit by a full-body shiver. I had seen Kay Stein, my realtor and friend, just the other day and had remarked how safe and secure I felt in my loft.

Now I felt violated. I was unnerved. Every sound made me jump. Each shadow hinted that danger lurked nearby. I understand that it's a normal reaction for anyone whose home has been broken into, but I wondered how long these feelings would last. I'd been in love with my place up until a few hours ago. Now…

I wanted a stiff drink, but needed to do my research before I was too wiped out to think. And it was Sunday…I was worried that the archives might close early.

CHAPTER 24

Ronnie, Lou and Nick

Sunday Evening

Lou stood up slowly and tried to work the kinks out of his back. He ambled over to the window and looked down on the lights of Atlanta. He wondered where Ronnie was. He was *afraid* to think about where Nick Escoba might be.

Five minutes later, he was still deep in thought when he heard a knock at the door. "Come," he bellowed.

Ronnie entered and shut the office door behind him. "Got some news that should interest you, boss. I did some more checking on Kate Jeffers. She works for Metro—freelances her services in some of their cases. Well-off, especially for a cop. That made me wonder, so I did some more digging. Her grandparents and parents were high society, Buckhead people. Dad was a prominent businessman here until he and his wife were killed in a car wreck...uh..." Ronnie paused, checking his notes.

"Thirteen years ago," Lou said, finishing the sentence. "Damn it! I knew I recognized that name! Jeffers. Elliot and Elinor Phelps

Jeffers. Killed when their car went through a guardrail. The cops said it was a single-car accident. Said Jeffers was speeding—lost control on the curve."

"Uh…yeah. You knew them?"

"Well, sort of," answered Lou. "I gotta talk to Nick. Anything else you need to tell me?"

"I got her file on them if you want it. Looks like the daughter, this Kate we're talking about, is looking into her parents' deaths. I haven't had a chance to go through all the stuff in here yet. You want me to take it or leave it here for you?"

"Yeah, Ronnie, leave it here," Lou said, absently. "I'll get back to you after I talk with Escoba."

Where is he, anyway? Lou asked himself as Ronnie placed the file on the desk and quietly exited. *He should be here by now.*

Lou went back to his desk and looked at the file for a few minutes, disturbed at what he read. He couldn't sit still and was pacing the floor, agitated, when Nick Escoba finally arrived. Lou wanted to bitch at him, but he knew better. Lou knew who was boss.

"Lou…just got into the city. Traffic is murder out there. Looks like your bar is doing a booming business. I stuck my head in for a second before coming up."

"Business is good," Lou answered, but his mind was elsewhere. Lou stopped pacing and faced the South American. "Nick, we've got a potential problem."

"What's that?"

"Remember that accident we had a long time ago…when the other car went down that ravine? Well, it may just come back to bite us."

"How do you figure? That was years ago and they closed the case." Nick sat down in one of the leather arm chairs and cut the end off a cigar.

"There's no statute of limitations on homicide. The daughter is poking her nose into things and, from the looks of this file of hers; she may be able to tie us to that night."

"*Us?*" said Nick, puffing on the Cuban. "I think we decided to say *you* were driving that night. As far as anyone's concerned, I was nowhere near here. Hell, for all they know, I wasn't even in the country. I may have been the one who drove them off the road," Nick continued. "But *you* were the only one who ended up in the hospital…leaving a paper trail! At any rate, we were long gone before the cops showed up…there's no way they can finger us."

Lou complained about finding his own name in the file.

"Fine, Lou. If you think she's figuring things out, you know what to do. Get rid of her. Or are you getting soft in your old age? I can always send one of my boys if you can't handle it."

"No, Nick. That's not a problem. I'll take care of her if necessary. I just thought we were in the clear after all this time, and then tonight I find out that this Kate Jeffers has had a file on us for a couple of years."

"If the information's been in there *that* long, she probably hasn't made the connection and chances are, she won't. Quit worrying!"

"Worrying has kept me alive for a good many years. I can't afford to get sloppy."

"Yeah, I hear you." But Nick didn't seem worried. He continued to puff on his cigar while he and Lou discussed some other business.

After Nick left, Lou called Ronnie on his cell. "Find out what else Jeffers knows and get back to me. We may need to eliminate her."

CHAPTER 25

Kate at the Archives Center

Sunday Evening

I squirreled myself away in the reference section, amid the stacks of magazines, newspapers and encyclopedias. I sat at a computer in a little cubicle and began pulling up microfilm copies of news clippings from years past.

I needed to get some information on the Bryants, on Ronnie Walker and on Lou Mancini. I needed to try to recreate my parents' file to figure out how much Ronnie (and lord knew who else) knew.

There were references to football teams and debutant cotillions. There were lists of those students making the headmaster's list each term. There were articles of weddings, complete with members of the bridal parties. I knew I'd find Emerson Bryant in here somewhere.

Arlington Bryant and his future wife, Penn Allister had graduated from *the* foremost private high school twenty-three years ago. They had both attended the state university, where they were members of a fraternity and sorority, respectively.

Emerson, three years younger, had followed in his brother's footsteps. He'd started at State twenty years ago, but ended up in the hospital after an "accident" at a frat house—the same fraternity that Arlington had joined. That's when things started heading south for Emerson.

Arlington and Penn had graduated the following spring. Their names were in the list of grads in May of that year. They'd married a couple years later.

The only time I came across Emerson's name after his freshman year at State was when he'd been arrested for DUIs, or had been released from different area clinics.

Wow, only the best lawyers and hospitals for this *boy.*

While I was sitting there, I had another vision. This time, as my eyes were getting blurry from scanning the microfilm, a big building popped up right in front of my eyes. I could see that it was tan-colored, on a busy street and there was a parking area on the right side. The vision only lasted a couple seconds, but it was very clear. Too bad I couldn't see a street number or a sign out front! Yeah, right! Even *I'm* not *that* good!

I grabbed my cell phone from my bag, punched in Carlos's number, and prayed for service. I was on the second floor of the library, so there was a chance.

"Hey, guys. It's Kate," I began when he picked up. "I just had a hunch. It kind of goes along with the vision I had Saturday morning. Are there any warehouses in Ansley Park?" I described what I'd "seen".

"No, not in the Park. None close by. But there *are* some over on Monroe. You know, south of the police station. And there's that area on Piedmont that has some storage units. We'll head over that way when we're through here at the Bryants' and see what we can come up with. Thanks, Kate. We'll check back with you later."

I continued looking at the microfilm. This time, I focused on the events of thirteen years ago. I had been twelve at the time. I looked up the account of my parents' accident. I looked up hospital admitting records, and anything else I could think of that I'd included in my file. I printed out everything. There *had* to be a clue in here somewhere or Walker would never have taken the file.

Next, I looked up info on Ronnie Walker. I didn't find too much. He'd been caught a couple of times for breaking and entering. Once for possession of stolen goods. Who knows what he did before he was "of age"! He'd lived with Lou Mancini for years—no relatives. "Interesting…" I mumbled aloud and wondered what *that* was about.

In checking out Mancini, I found that we'd been watching him for a number of years. He'd been involved with a South American drug guy—Escoba—who'd been deported a couple of times. But Mancini had never been officially charged with anything. He'd never done time.

Mancini had ended up buying a run-down building and fixing it up into a club a few years back. Appears to be a respectable place, at least on the surface…Prosciutto's.

"Yes!" I said aloud and quickly looked around to see if I'd disturbed anyone else who was working. That's the one I'd just driven past. I'd never been inside.

All of a sudden, I became woozy. My head started spinning. Yuck. At first I thought it was from reading all that tiny print zooming around on the screen in front of me, but then I looked at the clock on the wall. It was 9:30 already, and I hadn't eaten a thing. I needed to get out of here.

I gathered my things and returned all the stuff to the reference desk. I took the stairs to the main floor (you see, I *do* exercise) and headed outside.

I decided to call Grandma Jeffers to see if I could spend the night with her. I hated to impose and call this late, but she's a night owl and eats dinner "continental" style—at nine or ten in the evening. Maybe I'd get lucky and she'd fix us something.

And, of course, I needed to pick her brain and find out what she could remember about the Bryants.

"Sure, come on over!" she said. "Just beep your horn when you get to the gate, and I'll open it for you.

"Have you eaten?...No? Well, I've got plenty of food. You've got a dress and nightgown upstairs, so hurry along. See you shortly."

I was so glad I'd called! I didn't think I could face finger print powder at the moment.

Or maybe I just needed some nurturing. She was the one I'd always turned to—ever since I'd been little. Even when my parents had been living, Grandma Jeffers and I seemed to have a special bond. She understood me better than anyone else. I remember as a kid feeling 'different' from the rest of the family—sort of like I'd come from somewhere else and didn't quite fit in.

CHAPTER 26

Grandma Jeffers

———— ● ————

Sunday Evening

The aroma of comfort food hit me as soon as I walked in the door. I felt like I was six years old, coming to spend the night with Grandma. The fact that she didn't live in the main house any longer wasn't an issue. The gate house was toasty, homey and my problems seemed to melt away. "Oh!" I sighed, and started to drool. Quickly, I slurped up the errant saliva. "What smells so good?"

"You sounded like you needed something tasty, so I decided to whip up some baked macaroni and cheese for you. It's been your favorite dish, ever since you could crawl.

"I'm having some cabernet," she continued. "Would you like some? I'll pour a glass for you while you dress for dinner."

There's something about my grandmother that makes "dressing for dinner" all right. No matter how terrible a day I've had, the ritual of coming home, cleaning up for dinner, sitting with a cocktail, and discussing the day's events in a proper, refined fashion seems to help put things in perspective. The formal atmosphere where rules control behavior seems to impose a logic that is missing out on the streets.

I crawled, literally, up the stairs to the guest room. Gate houses are tiny! I don't think the upstairs was ever intended for real use. They were built generations ago when people were smaller than we are today. The stairs are steep and narrow. Getting up usually isn't a problem as long as you crawl, but coming down, especially in a dress, is a hoot! If I happen to have heels on, I have to sit on my bottom and bump down one step at a time. Perhaps that's another reason I feel like a kid again when I'm here.

I dressed for dinner. I keep a slinky black cocktail dress in the closet of the guest room and I slipped it on. I put on some heels (not very high...I can't do stilettos, like Glory) and...Voila! Instant transformation! The men in my life should see me now, I thought. Rob would be sorry...and Papa would...well, never mind! I bumped down the stairs. When I finally arrived at the bottom, I stood up, straightened the dress which had slid *all* the way up and attempted to become an adult again. In Grandma Jeffers' sitting room, my balloon wine glass was filled to the proper height. The glass sat on a pie-crust candle stand, (with a coaster, of course) in front of the stacked stone fire place.

The gate house that Grandma had moved into after Dave and Sarah's wedding was small, but cozy. Grandma had brought some of her favorite furnishings from the main house; antiques, mainly from the Queen Anne period. She had also brought several oriental rugs and some Chinese table lamps. The effect was almost "clubby", but still feminine.

I curled up in a crewelwork wing chair, after having slipped off my shoes. If the weather had been just a bit cooler, and we could have had a fire.

"Have some hors d'oeuvres while dinner is in the oven, Kate, dear. I was sorry I was unavailable for dinner at the big house last night, but it sounded like you young people had a fine time without me.

"Susan and I had the symphony benefit dinner on our calendars for quite some time," she continued. "I couldn't let her down."

Grandma joined me in the sitting room and tilted her head slightly, peering at me in her very 'knowing' way. "Now, tell me. You sound and look so tired. What is going on in your life that has made you so weary?"

I sighed, took a deep breath, and began. "It's been one of those days, Grandma. Actually, the past couple days have been difficult. I'm working on a case in which an eight-year-old boy has been kidnapped. I've had several visions, but they don't seem to tie in. I'm inclined to think it's an inside job, but can't get a handle on it. In fact, Grandma, you know the family. It's Penn Allister Bryant's little boy."

"Oh, my! Go on..."

"After I left Dave's last night, someone tailed me down Peachtree. I couldn't get a make on the car and when I turned off, they followed." (I neglected to give the hairy details of illegal U-turns and screeching tires.) "But I lost them, so that was cool.

"Then, today, Robinson Abrams and I went out for lunch..."

"Excuse me for interrupting, but he's that architect that re-did your loft, isn't he? It's so hard for me to keep everyone sorted out."

"Yes, and we've sort of been seeing a little of each other. But, without going into gory details, let's just say that the relationship thing didn't work out, so I doubt I'll be seeing *him* anymore.

"Anyway, when I got back to the loft, someone had gotten into my apartment and had gone through my files. I thought at first that it had something to do with one of my cases at work, but then I wasn't so sure. The guy talked his way in by saying that Rob Abrams had sent him! I don't see how they would even know each other. And *then* it turns out that there was just one file missing."

"Which was it?" Grandma knitted her eyebrows together.

"I had a file on Mom and Dad. You know I never believed that Daddy was a reckless driver. He wouldn't have driven off the road like they said."

"Now, Katie, dear. I know we've been through this before, but sometimes we just have to accept..."

"No, Grandma, hear me out. I think I'm on to something. The guy took *that* file. It was the only thing missing. Why would it be gone unless there was something in it that someone wanted kept quiet?"

"You do have a point. The officers at the scene weren't able to recreate the accident exactly. I remember them saying there *could* have been a second car involved. But your parents' car was so badly damaged..." Her voice trailed off, sadly.

"Grandma, I'm sorry. I know it hurts you to talk about it. That's why I've never said anything about the file. Dave and Emily don't even know about it. I started keeping all the information I could find on that day. Police records, hospital lists, newspaper articles, anything. I hoped that some day I'd be able to look at all the information and put my mind at rest. I can't accept that Daddy would have driven over the edge and killed Mom and himself. He would have been more careful!"

"I don't know..." Grandma sounded weary, herself. We sat in silence for a few minutes, each with our own private memories.

I straightened up in my chair and continued, "What's more, tomorrow is Monday. The ransom for Penn Allister and Arlington's son is supposed to be paid Tuesday, and we're no closer to solving it than we were two days ago! And since I've been so busy with all this other stuff I haven't even been back over to the Bryants' since yesterday morning. I feel guilty about not doing more to help out on the case."

"Maybe you should get out of the police business, Kate. I worry so much about you out there on the streets. Atlanta is a tougher town than it was when I was growing up."

"I know, Grandma, but I'll be all right. I'm not 'on the streets' like I used to be."

I followed Grandma Jeffers to the kitchen and helped her finish dinner. We grilled thick lamb chops and put together a salad. She took the bubbly macaroni and cheese out of the oven.

"I'm not quite as formal as I once was," she said and smiled. "We'll serve ourselves out here and then take our plates into the dining room, if that's all right with you."

I poured each of us another glass of wine and assured her I'd be fine without any servants attending us.

I concentrated on my food. Our lamb chops were pink inside, juicy and delicious. The macaroni had crunchy, buttery bread crumbs on top and was creamy underneath.

I bet I could learn to make this.

"You know..." Grandma said thoughtfully, during a lull in the conversation, "I think I heard something at the symphony dinner the other night. Something about Arlington Bryant's brother. He's in debt up to his ears again or some such nonsense. Now who was telling me that...?"

"What's the story on him, anyway?" I asked when it became obvious that she didn't remember with whom she'd spoken. "He was at their house when I arrived on Friday night. He looked like hell. Oops. Sorry."

Grandma, lost in thought, didn't notice my faux pas. "Oh, there was something that happened to him in college. Some kind of accident. That was years ago. I remember his parents being very upset and then...he was never quite the same afterwards. He drifted from job to job and took up gambling or something. I don't really remember."

Suddenly, I wasn't nearly as tired as I'd been. She'd confirmed what I'd found out from the papers. Was Emerson Bryant the man in the fetal position from my vision? Was that the connection? I was getting excited. That's it! He was in deep, and I was going to prove it!

But how is all this tied to my parents? What is the Mancini connection?

Grandma didn't know much more than that. Of course, I couldn't expect to get the answers that easily. But daylight was beginning to dawn in my little brain.

Our conversation turned to my sister, Emily. When I expressed my concern and the unusual vibes I'd been getting from her, Grandma Jeffers agreed.

"She seems more distant than usual, I have to admit. But she *did* break it off with that difficult artist she'd been seeing...and Sarah tells me she's begun dating a very nice young man—a landscape architect, I believe.

"You know, Kate, of all you children, it seems that Emily took your parents' deaths hardest. No, that's not what I mean to say. She *internalized* it more than you or Dave. You appeared to become more focused in everything you did: more serious. You concentrated on your studies; tried to use your powers of observation (I guess you call it psychic powers) to help people. And then you developed such a serious and committed relationship with your nice, young man, Thomas."

I'm still caught off guard when anyone refers to Papa as Tom or Thomas. I don't know if I'll ever get used to that name. I also find it interesting that Grandma thinks of our relationship as serious and committed. I'm afraid she's just looking at this from my perspective, not Papa's. Who knows *how* he feels! He's hardly mentioned anything to me.

Grandma broke into my thoughts again. "Dave, on the other hand, began to follow us (your Grandmother Phelps and me) around like a lost puppy. It seemed that his main goal in life was to please everyone: as if his being the perfect little boy would convince everyone to live forever and never leave him like his parents did. Very sad, if you ask me."

I nodded in agreement. It seems like he is continuing this same mode in his marriage with Sarah. He aims to please. I can't think that Sarah would be upset or leave him if he were more assertive. And she doesn't appear to take advantage of the fact that he's so easy-going where she's concerned. She wants to please him as well. They seem to have a great relationship.

Aloud, I said, "At least he's not like that at work. I mean, he's always working hard to please his clients and the company. But it's not like he allows anyone to walk all over him. And he's firm with the people he supervises: demanding, but fair and consistent."

"True. Let's move into the living room for our port," Grandma said, getting up from the dining table. She continued talking as she poured the dark red liquid from the decanter on the sideboard. "Getting back to Emily: she just withdrew after your parents died. We tried everything we could think of to bring her out. Oh, we succeeded, to some degree. But she's still so quiet. She's got her art and that seems to be her salvation. But it doesn't get her...*talking* to people. And that fellow she was dating. So dark and moody. I'm glad he's not in the picture any longer."

I nodded again. "Yes. Dave and Sarah have met the new guy she's seeing and said that he seems real nice. Maybe things will start looking up for Emily. She's only got one more year at the Art Institute and then she'll be out on her own and earning money. That will definitely help her mental state. It's not like she has to worry about finances. Thanks to you and Grandma Phelps, none of us have those concerns. But I know she feels bad not *contributing*."

"All three of you felt that way, I know. And I understand. It's good to be self-sufficient. Your parents instilled a very strong sense of responsibility and work ethic into you children. We just tried to reinforce those values."

"And we're all three very grateful for all you and Grandma Phelps did—and still do—for us!" I pushed myself up from my wing chair and gave Grandma a big hug.

"But I have to admit," I added with a yawn, "that I'm pooped. Your good food is exactly what I needed and I love hanging out and talking with you, but I'm exhausted. Plus, port wine always makes me sleepy. Let me pop the dishes into the dishwasher, okay? And then I'm going to call it a night. I love you, Grandma." I kissed her on her forehead and moved to the dining room to clear the table. I promised myself that I'd go to the Institute to visit Emily very soon.

CHAPTER 27

Kate

─────── ◆ ───────

Monday Morning

I woke up before dawn. Quickly, I slipped on my clothes and made the bed. I could hear the wind blowing around the eaves of the gate house.

I smelled coffee brewing as I bumped silently down the stairs.

Grandma Jeffers is old-fashioned in some ways, but has the latest appliances. She wasn't up yet, but had programmed the coffee-maker to start at 5:30. Bless her heart!

I curled up on the couch—a camelback, with my cup of coffee and wrapped up in a yummy chenille throw. I pushed the remote on the T.V. and then the 'mute' button (no need to wake Grandma.) and checked out the weather forecast.

The Indian summer weather we'd been having was over. The day was going to be overcast and breezy, a foreshadowing of the winter days to come.

I, however, wasn't going to be deterred by the weather or anything else today. I was rested and I had a plan! I finished my coffee and wrote a quick note of thanks which I left next to the sugar bowl.

I scurried to my car and headed down to Midtown and my loft. Everything was as I had left it. Walker had *not* returned during the night. I jumped into a wonderfully warm shower and washed my hair. After yesterday, it was about to get up and wash itself!

My hair does this 'fuzzy' thing right after I wash it—especially if the day is windy. So I decided not to mess with it. I blew it dry and pulled it back at the nape of my neck with a tortoise-shell clip. Black jeans, a medium-weight chocolate turtleneck, and low black boots and I was ready to go. Well, almost. I returned to the bathroom and applied blusher, mascara, and lip gloss. I didn't want to scare anyone.

I donned my suede jacket, grabbed my big black bag, remembered my cell phone this time and headed for the elevator.

Glory was already at the desk when I got to the parking garage. "Hey, girl," she said. "You're lookin' a little better than last time I saw you.

"I see you were gone all night. What happen? Did you hook up with some cutie-pie?"

"Yeah. My cutie-pie grandmother." I smiled.

"You going to let me ride with you today? I could leave my desk here, chase bad guys with you for hours, come back and no one would ever know I was gone."

"Not this morning, Glory. I'm a woman on a mission today. I've got a plan! I'm on to something, but it'd be boring for you. Just digging up more information. Wait till I'm *really* after the big boys, and then maybe you can come." I thought I'd humor her along.

"Be that way," she said, putting her nose in the air and pretending to pout. "All I've got to say is that there ain't *nobody* who messes with me and with all you've been through the past couple of days, you'd be smart to take me along with you—for protection, if nothing else! Why, I can distract anyone and I could get you out of trouble in no time!"

I closed my eyes for a second and could picture it—Glory "saving" me from all sorts of bad guys with a mere jiggle of her top! Actually, it would probably be very effective!

"Hey, did you talk to Ronnie Walker yet? Did they haul his sorry tail into the station last night?" she asked.

"Not that I've heard. But I'm on my way there right now. I'll find out. You know, we'll need you to identify him when we catch up with him."

"Really!? All *right*! I'm on it. I'll be ready. You can count on me. Now you go, girl…you go get 'em!"

How's that for someone cheering you on? Her enthusiasm was contagious. I hopped in my car, totally psyched, and headed to the station.

Carlos and Amy, primo detectives, were in Whitaker's office when I got there. I nodded "good morning" to all of them and sat down.

Whitaker was talking. "…got another call from the kidnapper. The money is supposed left on the parking deck in F Terminal at Hartsfield by 6:00p.m. Tuesday."

"That's a huge parking structure!" interjected Carlos. "Do we know where exactly?"

Whitaker nodded and continued, "As you all know, the Maynard H. Jackson, Jr. Terminal—Terminal F is for International flights, so we have to consider the possibility that the kidnapper will try to skip out of the country after grabbing the money."

"If that's the case, Lieutenant," asked Amy, "How do they release Eddie? Do you think they have another person working with them?"

"I don't know. The guy on the phone said they'd call the Bryant home as soon as they'd counted the money and let us know where to find the child.

"Kate," Doug Whitaker continued, looking my way. "What is your take on things? Any more visions?"

"I'm still trying to make them make sense. I'm convinced that it's an inside job. I've gotten some information about Emerson

Bryant. I need to double-check but it looks like he's in debt again. I'm betting he was the guy in my vision. He may be trying to extort money from Arlington and Penn Allister to pay off his debts."

Amy added excitedly, "That makes sense. We found out last night that Arlington paid someone a *pile* of money five years ago—Emerson's debts."

"But why go to all this trouble?" Carlos wondered aloud. "Why not just go to Arlington again?"

I told them about my plan to talk with all the Bryants. I informed them about being followed Saturday night. I shared that the missing file was the one on my parents. I told them I'd prove the connection, somehow.

"All right," concluded Whitaker. "We're making some headway. I'm off to meet with Arlington Bryant about the ransom. Let's meet back here at 4:30 this afternoon to go over what we've found. Of course if there's anything new before then, we'll let everyone know. Thanks for all you're doing."

Doug Whitaker is a demanding boss, but he's genuinely appreciative of everyone's hard work. He was on the street and then a detective for enough years to remember what it's like. I think that's one reason he gets so much cooperation from his officers. He truly respects them, so gets respect and extra hard work from them in return.

Amy, Carlos, and I walked out together. I was headed back to the Bryant home and they were going to scour the area, looking for leads.

CHAPTER 28

Kate and Emerson

———— ● ————

Monday Morning

After our meeting with Whitaker, Amy, Carlos and I stopped at the coffee machine and then headed out of the station.

Ahhhh...caffeine. After a double-double, my brain kicked in gear again. This was going to be quite a day. I was planning to interview each of the Bryants and hadn't had enough time to decide how I wanted to approach it. I hate it when I don't have all my ducks in a row!

Emerson met me at the door. He told me that Penn Allister was resting—she'd been up all night. And Arlington had gone to meet the lieutenant at the bank to finalize setting up the ransom process.

It was obvious that he didn't want me to come inside. "Gee," I began, trying to sound innocuous. "I really need to talk to both of them. But I don't want to disturb Penn. I know she's got to be exhausted! Would it be okay if I came in and asked *you* a couple questions?"

"Oh…I've forgotten my manners…please," he lied and stepped aside, letting me into the foyer and out of the weather. "Penn was frantic, just waiting around, so she made some cinnamon rolls. I'll have some sent in. Go on into the sunroom—I'll be right there."

He came in, followed by a maid who carried a tray. "That's all, Anne. Thank you." She set the tray on the curly maple tavern table and left.

"May I serve you some?" I inquired.

I'm not particularly domestic, but I was well aware of what I was doing. I silently coached myself, *be nice and friendly. Take the subservient role. Let Emerson feel in control.* That's the way to catch someone off-guard.

The sunroom was warm and inviting, a nice contrast to the blustery day outdoors. We could barely hear the wind and Arlington had started a fire before leaving for the bank. Emerson and I watched the flames dance and chatted about nothing in particular.

When I sensed that Emerson wasn't feeling *too* threatened, I stopped the small talk and began to shift the conversation. "…So tell me about Eddie. You two are pretty close?"

He opened right up! "I love that kid! He's always been such a character…right from the beginning…he ought to be a stand up comic someday. A real smart kid, too. I'm crazy about Janie as well, but I just have a special connection with Eddie."

"You're not married? No kids of your own? You seem so tuned in to your niece and nephew."

Instantly, I wanted to kick myself. I saw him tense up and knew I'd hit a nerve. *Well, this could be really good…or really, really bad.*

"Nah…never found the right girl," he said, attempting to sound off-handed, but failing.

I decided to be blunt since I'd already pissed him off. "Emerson, I've been looking into things, trying to help find Eddie. I noticed that your life changed dramatically fifteen or twenty years ago. Could you tell me about that?"

"What are you? Some kind of shrink? What good do you think my talking about *that* will do Eddie? He wasn't even born then!"

I thought, *Well, well! Back to his defensive mode.*

"I've found in past cases that everything's connected. I have a hunch that someone took Eddie because of something that happened to you...or to Arlington...or to your family a long time ago."

Using my most placating tone, I continued, "I'm just trying to get a handle on the dynamics to see who would want to do this. I'm asking everyone lots of questions, even if they don't seem related. You never know when something will fit into the puzzle."

I pressed on. "I really don't mean to pry, but I know something happened during your freshman year in college and you ended up in the hospital. Would you mind talking about it?"

"Yes, I would mind. I'm not going there. If you need to ask me about Eddie, fine, but that's it!" Emerson stood, arms crossed defensively across his chest and looked out the window at Wenn Park. "I'm concerned about the Kiddo. Why can't you people just do your job and quit sticking your noses in where they don't belong?"

Crap-o, I thought. *I've lost him. Why didn't I handle this better?*

"Okay." I said aloud, deciding to back off. "What about Penn Allister and Arlington? Are they all right? Any problems with their marriage? Financial difficulties that you know about?"

"They're fine. They're the perfect couple...the perfect family."

I detected bitterness in Emerson's voice. *He's the key to this whole thing,* I thought.

"One more question, Emerson...I understand you were kind of hard up for money a few years ago and Arlington bailed you out. May I ask the reason?"

"God, woman! You don't back off, do you?" He spun around from the window and glared at me. If looks could kill, I'd be six feet under! Emerson visibly struggled to control the rage going on inside. "Okay. I had some debts. I was in between jobs and was boozing pretty hard and ran up some bills. He helped out. That's all."

"Are you working now?"

"No." He glared at me and then said bluntly, "That's it, lady. I'm leaving," and he grabbed his jacket and stormed out the room.

———

I quickly stuck my head around the sunroom door and got Gomez's attention. "Have someone follow him," I mouthed, jerking my head in Emerson's direction. Gomez nodded.

Returning to the sunroom, I heard the front door slam and watched out the window as Emerson tromped down the steps to his car, fists clenched.

Well, that went well, I told myself sarcastically. *Next?*

I took the tray to the kitchen and talked briefly with Anne, the maid. She'd only worked for the Bryants a short time and wasn't any help at all. Darn.

Knowing I'd need to come back later to catch Arlington and Penn Allister, I said farewell to Gomez and left.

CHAPTER 29

Kate

───── ✸ ─────

Monday Noon

I was excited about Emerson, even though our talk hadn't exactly gone smoothly. Or maybe *because* it had gone so badly. He was hiding something…a lot of 'somethings'.

I headed back to my loft to check over all my notes again. I needed time to go through all the clippings I'd printed out Sunday night.

Sally was on duty, so I waved and headed upstairs, lugging my big black bag.

I made a nasty face when I saw the fingerprint dust all over my desk. I tried to brush it off, but merely succeeded in smudging everything. Crap!

Ignoring the mess, I set to work. I didn't want to sound like an idiot at this afternoon's meeting and still needed to make time to speak with Penn Allister and Arlington.

I spread my stacks of clippings out on the desk and rolled my computer out of the closet. At least they hadn't gotten powder on *it*! I typed frantically and came up with a timeline:

20 years ago	Arlington Bryant Senior in college Frat member
Emerson	Freshman pledges frat
	Injured in accident
18 years ago	Arlington marries Penn Allister
	Jane born five years later
	Edward born ten years after marriage
15 years ago	Emerson arrested (2nd time) DUI Booze and Drugs
	Spends several months in rehab
13 years ago	I was twelve
	Both parents killed in accident
	Louis Mancini listed in newspaper— admitted to Grady same night as parents' accident

BINGO!! That's the connection I'd been searching for. I printed out my timeline, stuffed the rest of the notes back into my bag and flew out the door. If I hurried, I'd be able to access the hospital files from the databank, interview the Bryants and get back to the station for the 4:30 meeting.

But first...I had to eat! The cinnamon roll from earlier just wasn't going to cut it. Apollo's was nearby, so I popped in there for a sandwich and soda. The gyro meat, a combination of lamb, garlic and who-knows-what-else, on pita bread, covered with Tzatziki sauce really hit the spot. Do you suppose I could learn to make *this*? I've been told that I should stick with easier stuff when I first learn to cook, but it's soooo good! And it's Greek.

Okay. I'd been doing really well, concentrating on my job all day and not thinking about Papa. And then I blew it by eating a Gyro and...do you think maybe I've got a subconscious thing going on here?

CHAPTER 30

Kate and Penn Allister

---●---

Monday Afternoon

I decided I should talk with Arlington next, but he and Whitaker were in the library, discussing the details of tomorrow's ransom drop.

So I asked Penn Allister to come in the sunroom to talk. "I don't know what to tell you, Kate. I'm so upset. I have no idea who would do this. Why is this happening?!"

Even though she looked much better, I could tell Penn Allister was on the verge of going to pieces, so I decided to tell her about some of my ideas. Maybe throw her a bone to give her a little hope. "I'm not sure exactly what is going on, Penn, but we do have some theories…"

"What? Please, Kate," she pleaded, jumping on the word 'theories'. "No one's told me anything. I'm going crazy here!"

Anne brought in a plate of sandwiches and a pot of tea. Distractedly, Penn accepted a cup and a sandwich. I'll bet if

I asked her, she couldn't tell me what she'd eaten. While I once again went through the domestic motions of pouring and so forth, I said, "I've had some hunches over the past couple days, and I think the Eddie's disappearance is somehow connected to someone very close to the family. What can you tell me about Arlington's business associates...or maybe Emerson's?"

"Oh, we're *very* close to Arlington's partners. They'd never do *anything* to hurt us! Jared's wife, Linda, has been over a couple times and has been a doll to bring us food and Stephen and his fiancée have stopped by, too. He's the newest in the firm. They are so busy with the wedding details—it's in a couple of weeks—but they've been great.

"As far as company finances go, Arlington doesn't say too much, but I think they must all be doing all right. Surely I'd know if one of them were having major problems. I mean, Stephen just bought "His and Hers" Lexuses...they can't be too bad off."

"How about Emerson?" I none-too-gently prodded. "He told me he's between jobs again."

"Poor Emerson...He's such a mess...I don't know what we're going to do with him...But he'd *never* hurt Eddie! He loves him to death!"

I wanted to ask if that was a Freudian remark, but refrained. Instead I asked, "Can you tell me a bit about his trouble when he was in college?"

Penn didn't hesitate like Emerson had. I'm sure it helped her feel good to talk about anything with anyone. "There was some hazing prank that went wrong at the frat house. We hadn't been dating too long, so Arlington didn't tell me very many details. I *do* know that Emerson got hurt and ended up in the hospital. He got hooked on pain killers and that messed him up. I didn't know him that well back then—he's three years younger than we are, but I guess he's never been the same since. He can't hold a job for very long. He's been in and out of detox a couple times for both alcohol and drugs...The last time Arlington went to pick him up, he told him that that was it—no more help...he doesn't mean it, though."

"I noticed the other night…Friday…that he was having a drink." I ventured.

"Yes, he's been drinking pretty heavily again. He stays clean for a while, but then he's right back at it. I suggested we take all the liquor out of the house, but there's *no way* Arlington's going to put up with that!"

I made sympathetic noises but I felt like screaming! *I mean, really! You've got an alcoholic or druggie in the family and you still keep the stuff lying around in plain sight? How stupid is that? And why the devil do I have to be so damned diplomatic in this job?* Instead, I bit my tongue.

"But Kate," Penn said, breaking into my thoughts, "Emerson wouldn't hurt Eddie!"

"Maybe that's not the main idea here," I replied, thinking aloud. "Did Arlington actually *tell* Emerson that he wouldn't help him again?"

"Yes, but as I said, he didn't really mean it. He's been coming to Em's rescue for years. He wouldn't stop now."

"But could Emerson have believed him anyway?"

"Well…I suppose…"

"Do you happen to know where Emerson gets his stuff? Or maybe who he hangs out with?"

"No. He doesn't seem to hang anywhere but here. He's such a nice guy and the kids love him—don't get me wrong—I do, too, but I didn't know it was going to be a "package deal" when we married. Arlington…and Emerson, too. You know what I mean?

I made some sympathetic noises.

Penn, meanwhile, was looking into the hallway and saw the door to the library swing open. "Here comes Arlington. Talk to him. He's sure to know more than I do. And Kate, thanks for your help. We really appreciate it." She left the room rather unsteadily.

Left by myself, I tried to put together a theory. Emerson was out of work. He was in debt again. If he believed that Arlington wasn't willing to help him any longer, would he be desperate enough to try something like kidnapping?

CHAPTER 31

Kate and Arlington

———◉———

Monday Afternoon

I stood as Whitaker and Arlington came into the sunroom. "I'm headed back to the station, Kate. I'll see you at 4:30, right?"

I assured him I'd be there.

Penn Allister walked Lieutenant Whitaker to the front door as Arlington sat down, motioning for me to join him.

"Thanks for giving me a few minutes, Arlington," I said in as friendly a tone of voice as possible. I was still feeling pissy about them being enablers for Emerson's addictions. If what I thought was true, they may have just been *asking* for something to happen to poor Eddie!

"I know how stressful this must be for you," I began. "You're one who seems to be in control of every situation, at work as well as at home. This has to be getting to you."

"Boy, you hit the nail on the head," he replied as he sank further into the chair opposite mine.

"Do you mind if I stir the fire and put another log on while we talk?" I asked, innocently. I wanted to be the one to take control this time. I needed to convince Arlington that I was on top of things, even if I didn't feel that way inside.

When he answered in the affirmative, I stood and poked at the fire. "I have some theories about what's going on here, but I need your assistance and cooperation if I'm going to be able to help out."

"Shoot. What do you want to know?"

I sat back down and looked directly into Arlington's eyes. I could tell he was a "get to the bottom line" kind of man, so I decided the direct approach would be best.

"In doing some checking, I noticed that you've bailed Emerson out on occasion when he's had financial troubles. Penn mentioned that you'd told him you weren't going to do that any more, so my theory is that Emerson is somehow behind Eddie's disappearance. If you could tell me about the hazing incident in college, it would be helpful."

When he looked thoughtful, I continued, "I also need to know who he deals with when he needs to get drugs. Whom have you paid off previously?"

Arlington sat quietly for a minute, then leaned forward and picked up a sandwich. Apparently, he made his decision to talk. Thank goodness, because if this approach hadn't worked I was in trouble. I'd run out of ideas!

Arlington stared at the sandwich as though the answers could be found inside. "Okay, I'll tell you what I know. Emerson pledged our fraternity his freshman year. I was a senior. The guys who were in charge of hazing got out of line. Things got out of control pretty quickly and Emerson got hurt. I was there for a few minutes, in the basement of the frat house. I looked in on him and he was practically passed out on the floor. He was heaving his guts out. I thought he was drunk. I figured he'd sleep it off and be fine, so I left. I remember I had a midterm the next morning so I went back to my room and studied. As a senior, I'd outgrown all the silly freshman binge drinking and partying.

"Next thing I knew, my dad appeared at the frat house and all hell broke loose! He was cursing and yelling like I'd never seen before and he threatened everyone in sight. I didn't know what was going on. Then he told me that Emerson was on his way to the hospital and said to get myself out to the car and go with him."

"How serious were the injuries?"

"They never actually said, but I know he was in a lot of pain and that's when he got hooked on the drugs. Even after he got out of the hospital, he was in so much pain that it was impossible for him to function. He ended up dropping out after that semester and just bumming around.

"Dad was so pissed. At him…at me…at the university. I think that's what really killed him in the end. He died a couple years later."

"I remember," I nodded, truly sympathetic. "I know Emerson has tried to straighten up a time or two, but can't seem to keep clean. Who does he get the stuff from?"

"I'm sure he has several sources, but the one I had to pay off about five years ago was a guy named Ron something-or-other… worked for some sleaze-bag club owner in downtown Atlanta. I think he's still around. The club was a legitimate business, but was also a front for a lot of undercover crap that was going on. I don't remember the details, but a couple of interns in our firm tried to dig up the dirt on the guy a couple of summers ago. He was connected to some big boy from South America, but they couldn't pin anything on either man."

Arlington looked up. "You think this is what we might be dealing with here?" When I nodded, he grunted, adding, "I hadn't considered that."

I couldn't sit still any more. I felt as though I'd drunk a gallon of high test coffee. I was finally onto something, and the adrenaline rush about made me nuts.

"Thanks, Arlington," I said quickly as I jumped to my feet. "You've been really helpful. We may be getting a handle on this. I've got to check into some other things. And I've got some pictures I need you to have a look at. I'll get back to you as soon as I can." And I practically mowed him down getting out of the room. I grabbed my bag and raced down the front steps to my car.

CHAPTER 32

The Warehouse

---●---

Monday Afternoon

"Joey, I'm bored," Eddie whined. "We've been here forever...I want to go home."

"It shouldn't be too much longer. You've been real cool about all this so far. Just hang in a little while more," Joey replied.

"You know," Joey continued, "it *has* been a long time. I'm beat. While you're sleeping at night, I'm keeping watch. I'm about dead on my feet."

"Do you suppose we could take a walk around in the main warehouse? And I need another bathroom break."

"First, let me check to make sure everyone has gone home." Joey unlocked the office door which opened into the main warehouse and looked around. "The coast is clear. Let's go, but you still need to be careful walking around. Some of these stacks of goods might not be too stable."

They walked to the workers' dining area, where the restrooms were. Joey stood outside while Eddie went in. Eddie'd looked before. No windows…no way out. When Eddie came back out Joey offered to buy him another drink. Then they headed back to the office area. Eddie tried to see what was written on some of the boxes that were stacked practically to the roof. He could make out a few words, but the light was so dim, it was difficult.

Safely locked in the office again, Joey stretched his muscles and rolled his neck from side to side. "I'm not used to sitting all the time—I bet you aren't either."

"Yeah, I'd even rather be in *school* than just sitting in here," Eddie replied.

"You want to play cards some more?" Joey asked.

"Nah, we played all day yesterday. But thanks, anyway. I'll just hang out on the sleeping bag." Eddie flopped down onto the floor with a huge sigh.

Joey settled himself in the comfortable desk chair and before long began to nod off. His head lolled back against the wall and soon he was snoring softly.

Eddie, however, was wide awake. He looked at Joey, asleep in the chair, and wondered where he'd put the keys. Eddie crept over and noticed a small lump in Joey's left-hand pants pocket. Disappointed, Eddie sat back on his haunches. There was no way to get a hold of the keys without waking Joey up.

Eddie's eyes strayed to the desk. Maybe there was another set in there. As he was trying to figure out how to get the drawer open, he noticed Joey's cell phone in his shirt pocket. It was barely peeking out. Eddie crept beside the chair, his heart hammering. Holding his breath, he slowly stood up. He could just see over Joey's shoulder. Carefully guiding his index finger and thumb, pincher-style, into Joey's pocket, Eddie was able to grasp it. Slowly, he pulled the phone from Joey's pocket. He lifted it over Joey's shoulder and sank back down to the floor, weak with relief. His heart pounded and his palms were sweaty.

Eddie gave himself a minute to let his heart slow down. Whom to call, he wondered. His mind was spinning. He tried to remember the phone number at home, his dad's office number, his mother's cell number…couldn't! "Think!!" he silently yelled at himself, "Think!" The only number he could remember was Jane's cell. He cupped the phone in his hands, trying to be as quiet as possible as he pressed the keys. He cringed and glanced in Joey's direction at each "beep" of the phone. Huddled in the furthest corner, he whispered when Janie answered.

"Jane…it's me, Eddie."

"Oh my god," Janie yelled. "Where are you? Are you okay? Speak up. I can barely hear you!"

"I can't…the guy's sleeping. I don't know where I am. We're in this big warehouse place. It only took us a few minutes to drive here the other night. Some of the boxes have like…food labels on them, but I can't see real well.

"Yours is the only number I could remember. I wanna come home, Jane."

"Did you call 911?" she asked.

"Uh…no. I didn't think about that."

"Well, hang up and call them. I'll tell mom you called and what you said. But the 911 people can trace your call. Hurry."

Eddie pushed "end" to disconnect. Just as he started to press the "9" key, the phone rang. Both Eddie and Joey jumped and yelped. Joey reached for his phone in his pocket, a bit disoriented from his nap. When it wasn't there, he looked at Eddie, curiously. "What…?" he began, but the phone rang again.

"Here," Eddie said and quickly thrust the phone into Joey's hand.

Joey answered, grabbed the keys from his pocket, unlocked the dead bolt, and stepped outside to talk. Eddie heard him relock the door behind him and sank, shaking, into a heap on the sleeping bag. "I'm done for, now," he whispered aloud. "He's gonna kill me."

CHAPTER 33

Monroe Street Station

———— ● ————

Monday Afternoon

4:30 on the nose. I literally skidded into the room where Lieutenant Whitaker and Detectives Williams and Stevens were seated at the conference table. Perhaps not the most professional way to enter a room and begin a meeting, but I was really excited.

I slid into a seat and attempted to contain myself. I bit my lip in order to keep quiet and we all looked expectantly at Whitaker as he began. "Here's what we've got so far: Eddie Bryant—kidnapped: 6:30 Friday evening. Family was at the home except for his uncle, Emerson, who arrived shortly thereafter. Williams and Stevens arrived at 7:02. The first ransom call: Friday evening at 9:45.

"The second call came just after noon on Saturday. The caller seemed to be very familiar with our airport here in Atlanta, which leads us to believe he may be a local boy. Also, his accent puts him from this area. Gomez was able to track the call to Northeast Atlanta."

Whitaker moved on to review the background work we'd gotten on the Bryants. Arlington and the others in his law firm seem to be doing all right financially. Penn Allister inherited from her parents when they died (nothing of note there, they'd both been ill for years) and has invested wisely. Penn spends her time volunteering at the kids' school and doing fundraising work for some of the big charities here in town—the symphony, the High Museum, March of Dimes and Cystic Fibrosis.

Then he got to Emerson and his history of trouble. After his accident twenty years ago, he got addicted to booze and drugs and has been in and out of detox centers every few years. Five years ago and Arlington paid off Ronnie Walker.

"Kate had a vision of a large building with a parking lot at the side. That's where we stand this afternoon. Amy...Carlos...any update on that end?" Whitaker asked.

"There are you-lock-it places along Piedmont and we checked them out, but nothing popped up," Carlos began. "Just south of here on Monroe, there are a couple warehouses that match Kate's description. They are large enough to fit her description. We plan on checking them out after this briefing."

"Okay, Kate, it's your turn. You seemed pretty excited when you rolled in here—fill us in on what you've been doing since this morning," Whitaker said.

I tried to keep my excitement under control. I told them what I'd been able to glean from the archives.

"This morning I was able to interview Emerson. He's hiding a lot. He's very bitter about his accident and won't discuss his injuries.

"When I got here a few minutes ago, I pulled up some records from the Grady Hospital database. Mancini was admitted for a back injury due to an automobile accident the same night my parents died. The hospital filed a police report because Mancini hit a cement barricade pulling into the emergency room that night. Lots of damage to the wall and to the front bumper of Mancini's vehicle, but the police report added this: there was *other* damage to his vehicle as well—he'd hit something else…my parents' car…I'm sure of it!

"This afternoon, I returned to the Bryants' and was able to talk with both Penn Allister and Arlington, separately, of course. It turns out that Emerson's up to his eyeballs in debt again.

"My theory is that they're all tied together in this, trying to get money from Arlington."

"Very logical, Kate," Whitaker stated. "But this time, they've gone too far—kidnapping. Why resort to that?"

"Here's why!" I said excitedly. "I've saved the real kicker for last. Both Penn and Arlington confirmed this: Arlington told Emerson he wouldn't pay off any more of his debts. He said this the last time Emerson got out of rehab. And right now…Emerson is *that* desperate!"

We all sat quietly, absorbing that bit of news.

The meeting wrapped up on a high note. Things were coming together!

CHAPTER 34

Nick Escoba

Monday Afternoon

Nick Escoba sat in the airport hotel bar nursing his martini. The interior was shrouded in darkness and the place was empty this time of day. He'd chosen a small table in the back corner and, as always, sat with his back to the wall. As he watched the entrance, he considered his options.

Lou was supposed to meet him upstairs in a couple hours. Lou was getting soft...not a good sign. If he didn't take Jeffers out or he spilled his guts about the accident...

One option was just to ice Mancini now and be done with it. But that could be messy—more ways than one.

Then there was the Jeffers girl. How much did she know? Would she be able to connect them? She needed to be dealt with.

And Walker. He'd been with Mancini for years. They seemed pretty tight. How much did *he* know?

Christ! Was he going to have to blow away everyone in town?

Of course, he could just leave the States and not come back. No one except Prosciutto's crowd had seen him. And, since he'd used a fake name and passport...as far as anyone was concerned, he was still in his home country.

But he *liked* it here, continued to rake in the dough and wasn't about to let himself be controlled by anyone. No way would he consider the last option!

He finished his drink and decided to hit the sauna before Lou arrived. He needed to be relaxed. This would most likely be an ugly meeting.

CHAPTER 35

Kate and Janie

———— ● ————

Monday Afternoon

I left the station and sat in my car, deciding what to do next. Amy and Carlos were heading south on Monroe to check out the warehouses. Maybe I could meet with Jane Bryant. She hadn't been interviewed since Friday night. Perhaps she had remembered some other detail.

I went back to Westminster Terrace and climbed all those stairs again. I wasn't even panting by the time I reached the porch. This was getting easier...I just might get in shape on this case!

Anne, the maid, let me in and ushered me towards the library where the Bryants were sitting. But before we'd crossed the foyer, Janie tore down the stairs. "Mom!! Dad!! Where are you?"

Both Arlington and Penn Allister bounded out of their chairs and rushed to the foyer.

"Eddie just called on my cell phone!" she exclaimed breathlessly, grabbing the banister to keep from falling. "He stole a cell from some guy who's watching him. He thinks he's not too far from here…in a building for some grocery store or something. I told him to call 911 so they can trace the call."

"Janie, you're brilliant!" said her dad. "Come on in here. Officer Gomez is here. Tell Ms. Jeffers and her everything!"

Penn Allister looked like she was going to keel over, so I directed her back to her chair. "I'm just overjoyed …and overwhelmed. So far my baby is all right," she cried, covering her face with her hands. "This is the first time I've been hopeful in days!"

Janie recounted her conversation with Eddie to all of us. Unfortunately, the caller information on Jane's phone just read "unavailable"…no number. Bummer! Gomez radioed Lieutenant Whitaker while I grabbed mine and stepped to the foyer to call Carlos and Amy.

"This is super," Amy said when I told her. "This is just great! We'll check with the 911 operator, too, to see if they received Eddie's call.

"And listen to this, Kate…we've checked out a couple of warehouses here and are just about to check out the third one. It's *tan* and has the parking area on the *side!*"

Cool beans.

Returning to the library, I asked Jane if she'd mind talking to me privately.

"Sure…no problem," she said. We decided to go back up to her room…to keep tabs on her cell phone, if nothing else!

On the way upstairs, everything went green—very weird. *Was that a vision?* I asked myself. I've never had one like *this* before, if that's what it was. I held onto the railing for a second. Then it was gone, just as quickly as it had come. Shaking my head, I continued up the stairs and followed Jane into her room. She hadn't noticed my hesitation on the way up.

Jane was quite open with me. It was clear that she had a good handle on the family members. "We're all a bit strange," she began, and proceeded to give me a brief description of each. "Dad works. Period. Oh, he's around once in a while, and it's cool when he is. But being a lawyer—it's hard: long hours and meetings out the wazoo.

"Mom's cool. She's busy with all the charity stuff, but she manages to be here when we get home from school and all that. She's *way* overprotective—especially of Eddie: "her baby". I'd kill her if she called *me* that!

"Eddie's a funny kid—ya gotta love him. He's in la-la land most of the time, but he's smart. He drives dad crazy. Dad wants him to be a lawyer, like him, but Eddie's just not the type.

"Me? I'm a nerd. I love to read and go to school. I guess *I'm* more like dad than Eddie is. Hey, maybe *I'll* be the lawyer!" She giggled.

"And then there's Uncle Emerson—he's just plain out-of-it. It's like he doesn't even belong to us, ya know? He's always here, just hanging out. Mooches off dad all the time. I don't know why my parents put up with it…but, he's nice to Eddie and me.

"He said something a couple nights ago—Saturday, I think. About Eddie and his favorite sweatshirt. I didn't think anything about it at the time, but then I started wondering…how does he know Eddie's wearing it? When I was telling Detective Williams about Eddie, I forgot to tell him he had his sweatshirt on—I just said jeans and a white t-shirt. You see, he'd already gone outside to go to the park, and I tossed the sweatshirt to him as he was getting on his bike. No one saw him after that. Uncle Em wasn't here yet— so how would he know what he was wearing if he hadn't *seen* him with it on? You see what I mean?"

I responded, "Exactly! I'll update everyone when I go back downstairs. And Janie, you ought to keep that "lawyer" idea in mind. I think you'd make a good one! By the way, what color is Eddie's sweatshirt?" I asked as I headed out the door.

"Bright green…and it's a hoodie with one of those kangaroo pockets in front. He looks like a Saint Patrick's Day advertisement when he's got it on!"

Green…Huh! I'll be darned.

CHAPTER 36

Whitaker

Monday Afternoon

Officer Gomez radioed the lieutenant.

"What have you got?" he demanded.

She filled him in on Eddie's call.

"Too bad we weren't informed about the daughter's cell phone. We could have been monitoring that too instead of sitting here with our thumbs up...

"Anyway, was there a number listed?"

"No...it was a cell phone. But Sir," Gomez began.

"I know," Whitaker interrupted. "I know. This is good. I'll get Williams and Stevens on this right away."

"Jeffers is with us here, Lieutenant, and is talking to them right now."

"Great. Have Kate call me here on my private line as soon as possible."

"All right, Lieutenant...406...I'm clear," Gomez responded, including her Unit number.

Kate Jeffers called ten minutes later. Whitaker swooped down on the receiver on the first ring. Kate apprised him of her conversation with Janie Bryant *and* of the green sweatshirt.

"Good going, Kate. Keep it up," The lieutenant told her.

"Oh, Doug…Amy was going to call the operator to see if they got Eddie's call. Have you heard anything?"

"No…it appears he didn't make the call."

"I just got a knot in the pit of my stomach, Doug." Kate said, fear in her voice.

Me too, thought the Lieutenant.

CHAPTER 37

Eddie and Joey

———— ● ————

Late Monday Afternoon

Eddie stood up and braced himself, his back against the wall, when he heard Joey unlock the door. He steeled himself for the worst, which he felt was sure to come. He kept his eyes locked on Joey as the latter made his way back into the room.

"Hey, kid. Looks like we may get out of here tomorrow." Then he frowned, remembering, and added angrily, "What were you doin' with my cell phone, anyway? Huh?"

Eddie thought fast and said, "Uh…you were asleep and I was really bored. I didn't think you'd mind if I looked to see if you had any games programmed on your phone. But as soon as I picked it up, it rang." Eddie prayed that Joey would buy his story and wondered if he'd go to Hell for lying. He thought maybe under the circumstances, that God would forgive him just this once.

"Oh." Joey considered for a moment. "Well, I do have a couple of games. But wait…I can't let you play them. How would Mr.… uh…the guy who's supposed to call me get through?"

"Yeah, you're right. I hadn't thought of that. Sorry. I won't touch it again." Eddie breathed a sigh of relief. Joey believed him. Maybe he wouldn't kill him after all. At least not yet.

"I guess I dozed off, huh? I hadn't better do *that* again. He'd be really mad. He's bringing some food over for us in a little bit. And as I said, this might be our last night. You'll be able to go home and I'll get paid this time tomorrow. Hope so, anyway. You wanna play some cards, now?"

"Sure," Eddie replied weakly.

CHAPTER 38

The Airport Hotel

───────●───────

Late Monday Afternoon

The sauna had helped. Nick hadn't realized just how tense his shoulders had been, so he'd gotten a massage, too, killing time before having to deal with Lou Mancini. The guy was a pain in the ass.

When he heard the knock at the door, he peered through the peephole and then slid the chain and undid the bolt to let Lou in.

Without a word, Nick tightened the belt on his bathrobe and returned to his chair and the cigar he'd been about to light.

Lou followed.

"What's with this insane kidnapping? And what have your people found out about the accident?" Nick began, lighting up.

"I'm meeting with Walker in a little while—back at the club. He's going to give me an update."

"I told you before, I can't be connected to any of this and I wanted the money before I left the States. This whole thing reeks of trouble. It's gone on way too long. I can't waste any more time in Atlanta…I'm leaving…first thing in the morning. You'll need to wire me the money. You know the account—same one we've used before."

"Okay—we should have it by tomorrow night," Lou offered as he watched Nick closely, trying to judge the other man's temperament.

Nick puffed, making the room hazy.

"Twenty-four hours. If not…you and your boy will be dead, as will the girl…it's just that simple. Now, get the hell out of here, before I change my mind and blow you away right now."

After Lou left, Nick continued to smoke his cigar. *Yeah…I'm going to have to leave, all right. But not yet…I'll tie up the loose ends first…suppose I am going to have to blow away half this damned town before it's all over!*

CHAPTER 39

Amy and Carlos

Late Monday Afternoon

Carlos pulled their unmarked car into the parking lot of the beige warehouse just as Kate radioed.

Amy listened and then relayed, "Eddie's alive and just called his sister's cell phone. He thinks he's pretty close—kidnapper didn't take him too far from home. And he said he's in some sort of warehouse. This could be it, Carlos! The place matches the one in Jeffers' vision."

Carlos glanced at Amy. "You know, I don't put stock in any of this mumbo-jumbo, but I've got to say, she's been right-on before. If this pans out, I just might start believing!"

"Shall we check this place out?"

The radio squawked and Whitaker shouted, "Unit 426...Get back here, on the double. We just got a break in the case!"

"Yes, Sir," Amy radioed back. "But Lieutenant, we were just going to check out a warehouse here on Monroe."

"You're what…one minute south of the station? I'll send another unit. I need you here."

"We're on our way. 426…clear."

"Man," Carlos sighed, shaking his head. "I thought we might be onto something here." He fired up the car again and pulled back onto Monroe, heading north.

Amy called the 911 operator. Unfortunately, they'd received no call from Eddie Bryant.

CHAPTER 40

The Kidnapper

Late Monday Afternoon

"Shh…! Everyone quiet," hissed the man. "Someone's just pulled into the lot."

He slipped out the door and positioned himself so he could see the parking lot of the warehouse.

The car parked and it appeared that the couple was going to get out. Why would anyone be here at this hour? And why a woman? It made him nervous. He kept watching. They looked like cops— just something about them. They were talking and checking out the place.

Then, the engine started up again, and they were gone. "What the…?" he shrugged.

The man went back into the office. "Joey, I don't like this…it doesn't feel right. Somebody's sniffing around here. We'll need to move the boy…tonight. Let me figure some other place…I'll be back. Try to get this place cleaned up while I'm gone. I'll be back in say…fifteen minutes."

Joey nodded and the man left.

"Well Eddie," Joey said cheerfully. "I told you we wouldn't be here too much longer."

Eddie thought—yeah, but *now* where're we going? He was used to the office now. He didn't want to go somewhere else.

"C'mon. Help me carry these pop cans and stuff back to the cafeteria. You heard him—he'll be back soon."

Eddie grabbed a few cans and an empty chip bag and followed. One can slipped from his grasp and clattered to the floor.

Joey jumped at the racket. "Whoa there, boy. You tryin' to give old Joey a heart attack or something?" Joey chuckled and continued toward the cafeteria.

That gave Eddie an idea. "Let me just get the can that I dropped. I'm right behind ya, Joey." Eddie snatched up the can. Then he slipped between two rows of pallets. He tip-toed parallel to Joey, one row to his left. There were boxes stacked from one end to the other. Eddie spotted two tall stacks that looked like they were leaning slightly. As they passed the first, Eddie pushed the stack to test how easily he could move it. Not bad, he thought. If he pushed really hard on...the fourth box from the bottom...

"Hey, kid, you comin'?"

Eddie froze, rooted to the spot. He was afraid to speak...Joey would be able to tell exactly where he was.

"Ah, come on, Eddie. We don't have time for this...He'll be back soon."

Joey stood there, looking around. This was Eddie's chance. He threw himself at the second stack of boxes. He put his shoulder right where he wanted—the fourth from the bottom.

Joey was caught off-guard. As the tower of boxes tumbled on top of him, he dropped the trash he was carrying and sunk to the floor, dazed.

Eddie dropped the stuff he was carrying and ran the other direction, back toward the side entrance. He had to get out before Joey collected himself! Racing as fast as he could, Eddie hit the side door. It burst open and crashed into the side of the building.

He was free! He blinked in the light. The afternoon was cloudy, but Eddie was so used to the dim warehouse, the afternoon light blinded him. *Gotta get out of here,* he told himself.

He was in the parking lot. It was empty, but the other guy was going to be back any second. He looked around. The place was surrounded by a tall chain-link fence and there was nothing but another warehouse on the other side.

The street. That was his only choice. He'd be spotted for sure, but he didn't have any place else to go. Eddie took off running. He turned left out of the parking lot. He wasn't sure where he was, but it looked a little familiar. He checked the sky. You can tell direction by the sun. But the day was too cloudy. No sun.

A little further on, Eddie came to an intersection. "Monroe and Ponce De Leon," he panted aloud. "I've *heard* of them."

He paused and looked around, hoping to get his bearings. Ponce De Leon looked like it had houses down to the left. He decided to chance it. He didn't have much to lose.

CHAPTER 41

The Warehouse

---•---

Late Monday Afternoon

The squad car pulled into the warehouse lot and the officer instantly reached for his computer to send a silent request. "The side door to the warehouse is standing open," he typed rapidly. "No one outside and no one near the doorway. Send backup—no way should this door be open at this hour of the afternoon. I'm proceeding inside…256 clear."

The officer exited the cruiser and made his way cautiously to the open doorway. He peered inside, still saw no one, stepped into the warehouse and crouched down quietly. He listened and allowed his eyes to adjust to the dim interior.

After a minute, he could see relatively well. He noticed that the door to what appeared to be an office area was ajar. He made his way to the door, listened, and pulled it open, careful not disturb any prints that might be helpful to detectives. He noted the sleeping bag, rumpled on the floor next to a large brown wooden desk and swivel chair. There were some boxes scattered on the floor near one corner of the room. The only window was high up on one wall. The only other item in the room was a deck of cards on the desk.

As the officer was scanning the room, he heard a noise from the main area of the warehouse. Crouching near the door, he peered out and saw a large man approaching from behind the stacks of boxes. He was rubbing the back of his head and groaning. The man turned back around, looking behind him. He appeared to be unarmed.

"Police—stand where you are. Show me your hands."

"Oh, god!" cried Joey, reaching for the sky. "Okay…don't shoot!"

CHAPTER 42

Emerson Bryant

Late Monday Afternoon

He drove south on Monroe Street, past the Police Station. Not a lot of activity going on there. He chuckled and headed further south. A cruiser followed him from the station, so he was careful to obey all the rules. He was about to change lanes so he could turn into the warehouse parking lot when the cruiser sped up, passed him in the left-hand lane and signaled to turn.

There aren't any streets around here, just driveways, the kidnapper thought. Emerson Bryant frowned, wondering where they were headed. He moved to the left lane himself, leaving plenty of room between himself and the cops.

"Shit!" he exclaimed, realizing where they were turning. "They're going into the damned lot!" He drove slowly on past, thankful he hadn't been thirty seconds earlier. If he had, they'd have pulled in right behind him! As he passed, he allowed himself a quick glance. There were *two* cop cars! And the door to the damned place was wide open!

"Jesus Christ," he exploded. "What the hell happened?"

He changed lanes again, drove to the next intersection, and took a right onto Ponce De Leon. Two blocks down, he pulled onto a side street and parked. He was shaking. He needed a plan. He had to find out what had gone down at the warehouse. And, more importantly, what had happened to Eddie and Joey.

CHAPTER 43

Eddie

―――――――●―――――――

Monday Evening

Eddie passed by the first several homes. He wanted to put some distance between himself and Monroe Street. But he knew he needed to hide. The next house had two large brick posts, one on either side of a long driveway. Bushes hid the home from the street and the front lawn had lots of trees.

Perfect, thought Eddie. He slipped in next to one of the posts and crouched in the bushes. He was pretty sure he couldn't be seen from the house *or* the road and was glad that his sweatshirt was green. Not exactly the same shade as the bushes, but at least it wasn't bright orange!

Eddie sat for a while, catching his breath. When his muscles began to ache, he found a better hiding place, one where he could stretch his legs.

He felt bad about Joey. Joey wasn't a bad guy. He hoped he hadn't hurt him too badly. Eddie was sorry he'd had to topple the boxes on Joey; good thing most had been empty. But it had been his only chance to get away. They were going to move him—who knows where. Eddie admitted to himself: he'd been scared.

Maybe he'd be able to make it up to Joey somehow. After all, Joey'd been nice to him. *He* hadn't kidnapped him. He was just doing what the other man had told him to do. Joey'd given Eddie food and drinks and a sleeping bag. He'd talked to him and played cards with him. He'd trusted Eddie enough to let him out of the office once in a while and take bathroom breaks...*yeah, Joey was okay.*

Not the *other* one! He didn't even want to say his name! Why had he taken Eddie to the warehouse? Uncle Emerson had always been Joey's favorite person in the whole wide world. Now Eddie *hated* him! His uncle had always been nice to him...so much fun... until now! How could he be so great one day and so...*evil* the next? Eddie was confused.

He peeked out of his hiding spot.

It was going to get dark soon. He was hungry, cold and he didn't know where to go. Pulling his knees up under his chin, Eddie curled himself into a tight ball. He was trying to be brave, but he'd used up all his energy. Tears slid down his cheeks and he sniffed. He wiped his eyes and nose on his very favorite sweatshirt and he didn't even care!

CHAPTER 44

Prosciutto's

---●---

Monday Night

Ronnie and Lou sat at a corner table in the back of Prosciutto's. There was enough noise that they could talk and not be overheard. Lou wanted it that way.

"So...she checked the hospital records the night of her parents' accident and found your name on Grady's list." Ronnie continued, "I found the news clipping in that file Jeffers had. There were several pages of notes, but it doesn't look like she's made any real connection between you and her parents."

"Doesn't matter. She's got to be eliminated. I can't have anyone put us at the scene."

"There's no indication that she knows anything. Maybe we should just sit tight and wait to see what happens. I can destroy the file and try to find any other copies she may have made. I can always take her out later."

"No, let's do it now, while no one knows. We don't know if she's got other copies anywhere and there's no way we can alter the hospital and newspaper records. It's too complicated. If she found it once, she, or someone else, can come up with it again. I wasn't driving, but Nick has made it real clear that he will pin it on me, if pressed. No, it's best to do it now. Otherwise I'm a dead man, either by the police here or by Nick Escoba. He even said he'd take you and the girl out himself. Best to do as he says. NOW, Ronnie. I don't want to know details. Just do it."

"Whatever you say, Lou," Ronnie answered, skepticism in his voice.

Ronnie walked out leaving Lou brooding over his drink and wondering if the boy was getting soft on him.

Ronnie muttered to himself as he made his way out of the building. He shook his head. "Lou's getting too worried to be the boss anymore," he said. "I know I've been with him for a long time, but he's too damn jumpy. This Jeffers girl doesn't know he's connected—there's no way she can prove he was at the scene. I don't need her blood on my hands. I'm no chicken, but Lou's losin' it."

CHAPTER 45

Amy and Carlos

●

Monday Night

Detectives Carlos Williams and Amy Stevens were in their unmarked car, parked across from Prosciutto's when Ronnie left Lou's establishment and walked west on 11th Street.

"What do you think, Carlos?" Amy asked, peering at the man who was headed their way. "Is that he? White, about average height, muscular, medium-length brown hair."

"I hate to tell you, Amy, but you've just described forty percent of the guys in Atlanta," answered Carlos, smiling.

"Yeah, yeah. You're real funny."

"I'll try to control my sense of humor for your sake," teased Carlos. He captured a picture on the digital camera as Ronnie walked past. "All right, it's him. Let's stick with him and see what he's up to."

They kept back, but followed Ronnie as he made his way to a parking lot. He was mumbling to himself and shaking his head, apparently disturbed about something. Amy pulled to the curb as

Ronnie entered the lot. He went inside a small shack and was there several minutes.

"What is Walker doing in there, having his teeth cleaned?" remarked Carlos, impatiently. "He's taking forever! You didn't see him come back out of the kiosk, did you?"

Amy laughed, but squinted towards the parking lot, just in case. "We wouldn't still be sitting here, would we?! ...men! Always so impatient." Amy shot back, rolling her eyes.

Finally, Walker emerged and got into an older Chrysler. He pulled out of the lot. The detectives followed at a distance, keeping the car in sight.

"I'll check my instant messages. You keep your eye on Walker. Where do you suppose he's heading?" Carlos asked, more to himself than anyone else.

"Oh, my God!" Amy. "I'll be darned. He's parked across from Kate's garage! So now he's watching *her* and we're watching *him*."

"Just hope that no one is watching *us* while we watch *him*," Carlos remarked as he glanced around.

"No kidding," was Amy's emphatic reply as she settled in her seat to watch. "And, Carlos, you're starting up with the humor thing again."

"Oops...Sorry," Carlos replied, chuckling.

"You're sorry, all right...more ways than one."

CHAPTER 46

Joey

───────── ◉ ─────────

Late Monday Afternoon

"Don't shoot!" repeated Joey, flinging his arms into the air.

"Take it easy, fellow," said the officer, walking closer. "I just want to talk to you. I see you're not armed. Go ahead and lower your hands."

The officer radioed to cancel his backup. "Looks like a harmless vagrant," he added quietly.

The dispatcher called Unit 155.

"We're just pulling into the lot. Go ahead and talk to the guy. We'll stay here for a few minutes, just in case…155, clear."

The officer kept talking to Joey in a calming manner. He could see that the man was agitated. "Come on over here. We'll just sit on a couple of these boxes over here and you can tell me what you're doing here."

Joey complied, wondering what he should tell the policeman.

"First off, tell me your name," began the officer, pulling out his notepad and a pen.

"Why are you here in the warehouse?"

"I work here."

The officer was surprised, but noticed Joey's uniform. "You know I'll need to verify that."

"Okay," Joey replied.

This guy looked like he hadn't seen bath water for quite some time. The officer asked, "Why were you rubbing your head when I first arrived? Had something happened to you?"

"Yeah," said Joey, remembering. "I was taking some trash to the cafeteria to throw it out, and some boxes fell over and hit me in the head. It only hurt for a minute. They were empty."

"Let me ask you another question. Do you have a home?" he asked, thinking about the sleeping bag in the office.

Joey nodded and told him about his little apartment.

"Well then, Joey. What can you tell me about the sleeping bag I saw in the office?"

Joey hesitated. He didn't want to talk about *that*. He'd always been told it was a bad thing to lie—especially to a policeman. Instead, he said, "I stayed here last night. And that's not the office anymore. They moved it upstairs last year. It's just a room, now."

"I see. So you stayed here last night? Is that why you're here now—on a Monday—after work hours?"

"Part of my job is to keep an eye on things." Joey looked at the floor and scuffed a foot around, feeling embarrassed.

The officer smiled kindly, realizing Joey's mental capabilities. "I doubt if that means you need to stay here twenty-four hours a day. Why don't we just lock up…you have a key? And then I'll drive you home. How would that be?"

"Okay," answered Joey. He was glad the guy'd stopped asking questions. He really didn't want to get in trouble. He would be in enough trouble when Mr. Bryant found out Eddie had gotten away!

"Let's go to the cruiser and I'll verify that you're an employee. Then I'll run you home."

"Can I sit in the *front* seat…with you? I'll be just like a cop." Joey smiled, followed the officer outside and handed him the key to the side door.

CHAPTER 47

Ronnie

———————●———————

Monday Night

Ronnie was still muttering to himself as he got in his buddy's beat up Chrysler. Things were *not* going well. His boss was getting skittish. Lou was after *him* to do the dirty work, and Ronnie really didn't want to get involved with anything connected to that Nick Escoba dude. He'd seen people lose their kneecaps to guys like him. And anyway, this Gloria chick was really hot. He wouldn't mind...

He cruised over to 14th Street and parked once more, across from the entrance to Kate Jeffers' garage. He'd sit here a while and scope out the place. Maybe Gloria was working this shift. He wondered what his chances were with a girl like her. Or maybe she just flirted with *all* the workmen who came to the building.

Ronnie reached for the door handle, trying to decide what to do about Jeffers. Then he noticed a car that was pulling into a parking space several cars behind him. Looked familiar. Was he being followed?

"Man, you're good." Ronnie pulled his hand away from the handle, congratulated himself for being so alert and snorted. "Timing is everything!" He thanked his lucky stars he hadn't gone in there looking for Gloria or for Jeffers' car. Too hot a situation to go in there right now. Better to let things cool off for a while.

CHAPTER 48

Lou

———— ● ————

Monday Night

Lou was still at the back table at Prosciutto's. He waited until Ronnie'd had plenty of time to get to the car before launching his plan. He was depressed. He was going to have to handle things himself. No way was Ronnie going to go through with the plan to take out the Jeffers woman. He'd known the boy so long; he could read him like a book.

Lou had taken Ronnie off the streets when he was a kid. He'd raised him. Given him a place to stay. Taught him all he knew about the business. He hoped in return that Ronnie would be loyal, but realized now that he couldn't count on him—not for murder, anyway.

"God damn it," he muttered, shaking his head sadly. "I'm going to miss you, kid. But…business is business."

Lou slowly got out of his chair. He stopped to check with his manager before going up to his office. Things were going well, according to the manager. The cashiers were too busy to even take a break. The patrons looked happy and relaxed. Lou gazed wistfully at them. Not a care in the world, or at least it seemed that way. Where had he let things go wrong? "I'm getting too old for this job," he said under his breath. "There's just no pleasure in it anymore."

Once upstairs, Lou placed a call to Emerson Bryant's cell phone. Emerson answered on the first ring. "What's-a-matter? You feelin' jumpy?" he asked, not having to identify himself. Bryant would know who was calling.

"I can't talk now," Bryant replied sharply.

"Then don't. Just listen. I want the Jeffers woman to make the ransom drop. My man will count it and call me, understand? Once that's done, I'll give you the go ahead and you can do whatever you want on your end. The kidnapping was real stupid on your part, ya know? You could've come up with the money some other way…but that's *your* problem!"

Lou disconnected. *Then I'll take both Jeffers and Walker out myself when they leave the airport. Get the money, wire it to Escoba, and be done with this whole damn mess.*

Lou hobbled down the back stairs of his building and clambered into his car, breathing heavily.

Then he headed out after Ronnie.

CHAPTER 49

Ronnie

⬤

Monday Night

R onnie checked his mirrors as he pulled away from the curb. The unmarked car pulled out into traffic behind him. Ronnie felt nervous and checked his rearview mirrors every few seconds.

The car stayed behind him for several blocks. Then, all of a sudden, it made a right turn and disappeared down the side street. Ronnie realized he'd been holding his breath and exhaled slowly.

"You're a fool," he chided himself. "It's Lou. He's got ya all keyed up. The car was dark and the broad was probably just there by coincidence. No need to worry. It's like I'm an old man, like Lou. Gettin' soft in my old age!" And he headed to his favorite eatery— Pasta Mama's, to grab a bite and figure out what to do about the Jeffers girl.

Pasta Mama's was already crowded with happy, boisterous patrons. Ronnie, a regular, sat at a small table for two in the far corner, his back to the wall. Lou'd taught him to do that—a long time ago. It was instinct now. In fact, Lou'd taught him everything he knew over the years. But Ronnie couldn't waste time reminiscing. He was bummed that he couldn't relax and feel jovial like the rest of the crowd. He had some thinking to do.

Ronnie mumbled to himself over a beer while waiting for his food. "You know if you kill Jeffers, people are going to be all over you looking for answers," he reminded himself. "And if you're the one pulling the trigger, you're the one that goes down.

Nope, Lou's just plain wrong to want to get rid of her. Maybe I can just scare her off somehow or..." And Ronnie began to put together a plan.

———— ❊ ————

"He's onto us..." Amy said. "Keeps checking his mirror. Get someone to take over, quickly, Carlos."

But Carlos was one step ahead. He was already on the laptop, typing in their request. He liked to use the computer in situations like this. Too many bad guys have the equipment to hear the police radios. "426 needs an unmarked to take over surveillance..." he typed.

The reply came back in seconds. "Unit 276 is headed north on Glendale. They'll pick you up there.

Carlos noticed the unmarked car trailing them. Amy let them take over surveillance as she made a right onto Taft Avenue.

The new car continued to follow Walker and watched as he pulled into the parking lot at Pasta Mama's. The officers parked where they could watch both the old Chrysler and the front door.

Twenty minutes later another interesting vehicle pulled into the lot. "This is getting' good," remarked one officer to the other.

"Get on the horn and let Williams and Stevens know...Mancini just pulled in."

CHAPTER 50

Pasta Mama's

─────────●─────────

Monday Night

R onnie sat at Pasta Mama's and swirled the beer in front of him. He always thought better on a full stomach. "Lou's always had me doin' little stuff, breaking and entering, things like that. Been in a few fights, but nothing serious. I'm a big enough guy that all I ever had to do was look at someone and they'd back down. I've never killed anyone and I don't want to start. Not a woman. Not with someone who works with the cops. Hell, she even used to *be* a cop! No freakin' way I'm going to touch that! And she's Gloria's friend." He continued talking to himself. *You* can't *blow* that, *man. Come on, Ronnie, think! You need a plan.*

Ronnie looked up from his bottle as the waiter brought his food and was shocked to see Lou following the server. He sucked in air and tried to pull his thoughts together. Lou eased himself into the chair opposite. "Gotta do something about this back of mine," Lou wheezed. He pointed at Ronnie's beer and indicated to the waiter to bring two more.

When the beers were served, Ronnie began. "Lou, I stopped by Jeffers' building, but I think I was followed. It's too hot to move right now."

"If I'm reading you right...and I think I am, it's always gonna be too hot for you. You don't *want* to take out the girl," Lou started, getting angrier by the second. "Since when do *you* decide what's going to happen? Last time I checked, *you* were workin' for *me*," he added.

"Don't worry, Lou. I said I'd take care of it...I'll handle it, just not quite yet."

"Yeah, I saw the car, too. I followed *you* because I figured you'd be a pussy and not follow through."

"Wha'd'ya think...!" Ronnie began, but Lou interrupted.

"Enough!" Lou said sharply. He swigged the rest of his beer and slammed the bottle on the table. Ronnie was surprised the bottle hadn't shattered with the force. Lou was really pissed.

"I have to be able to trust my people," Lou hissed, leaning forward. "Wasn't I the one who took you in off the streets way back when you were just a snot-nosed punk? You forget about that? Don't you appreciate what I've done for you? Is this how you thank me for everything? I treated you like one of my own. Now you start thinking you're smarter than me. You start makin' the rules and doin' what you want, and you're a dead man, Ronnie. You hear me? If someone doesn't ice you first, I may have to do it myself!"

Ronnie looked into the face of the fat man as he levered himself out of the chair, and knew Lou meant every word he said.

It didn't take long for Ronnie to decide what he had to do.

CHAPTER 51

Ronnie and Gloria

---◆---

Monday Night

S hortly after leaving Pasta Mama's, Ronnie pulled the Chrysler into Kate Jeffers' parking garage. Again he wondered about his chances with Gloria.

As he approached the desk, she stood up, eyes squinting and hands on her hips. "That answers *that* question," Ronnie muttered unhappily. Then he squared his broad shoulders and put on his most charming smile.

"Just who do you think you are? Sashaying in here like you've never done anything wrong in your life. Let me tell you a thing or two...Max or Ronnie or whatever the hell you're calling yourself today.

"I'm in big trouble with Ms. Jeffers and the police—lettin' you sweet-talk your way in here the other day. Now you just wipe that grin off your face there, buddy—it won't get you past me tonight. No, siree, never again!" Glory bustled around the desk until she was toe-to-toe with him, hands still on her hips.

"Okay, buster, what name am I supposed to call you when I dial the police station?"

"Calm down. I don't blame you for bein' upset with me…"

"Upset? Upset?! I'm not upset…I'm pissed as hell! Tellin' me that you're Max, the painter. Comin' in here and getting Kate Jeffers's keys like you own the place. Telling me that *Mr. Abrams* had sent you…What a load of crap! And to think for a second I was taken in by you and that nice smile…"

"Whoa, whoa…hold on," Ronnie interjected when she stopped to gasp a quick breath. He raised both hands in an 'I give up' gesture. Even though he knew it would get him in more trouble, he couldn't help smiling. She was damn cute when she was riled up.

"As I said," he continued in a soft, soothing tone. "I don't blame you a bit. That was real bad of me to do that. I'm here to try to straighten things out. I'm hopin' to help, if you'll give me a minute to explain."

Glory backed down—slightly. "I'm listening. You're gonna tell me your real name, for starters." *Let's see if you can be honest about that!* she thought. "And then you're gonna tell me how you plan to "help out". Make it snappy. I've still got a mind to call the cops."

"All right. For starters, my real name is Ronnie Walker and I work for a guy named Lou Mancini—owns Prosciutto's. Well…I *used* to work for him—up until about fifteen minutes ago. I think I just got fired."

"What do you mean you "think" you got fired?"

"He didn't say flat out, but he threatened to kill me if I don't get Jeffers off his back."

"Well, Mr. Ronnie Walker, it appears to me that *you* are the one in need of help. How're you going to help *us* if you're lookin' to get your *own* self killed?"

"I guess I was hoping that we could help each other…you know, I'll let you in on what I know and you can put in a good word for me with Jeffers and the police."

"Hmmm. I'll need to give that some thought. *And* talk to Kate," Glory grumbled more to herself than anyone else. To Ronnie, she said, "What did this Mancini character have in mind for you to do with my friend Kate, anyway?"

"Take her out of the picture."

"Take her out...you mean *kill* her?! Why? What did she ever do to him?" Gloria started to bounce up and down on her toes, her breasts jiggling. Ronnie averted his eyes, trying to keep his mind on the subject. He tried to focus on what the woman was saying... "*Kill her?* I don't understand."

"I'll explain a little to you, but I'd prefer to talk to both you and Jeffers at the same time. You suppose that's possible?"

He briefly shared his ideas with Gloria.

"Well, my replacement is supposed to be here at the desk in just a few minutes. Will that do? Oh, here's Sally now. Lemme talk to her."

Ronnie sighed in relief, "Then would you call Jeffers and see if we can go up there? And I'm *not* asking you for the key," he added, shooting her his best grin again.

Fifteen minutes later, Glory and Ronnie were sitting in Kate's living room.

CHAPTER 52

Kate in the Loft

———— ● ————

Monday Night

I put on my favorite flannel pajamas, poured a bourbon and water, and headed for the garden on my roof. "This is the first time I've had one minute to myself!" I muttered. "I need a shower…a drink…some down time…sleep…!"

I never made it to the balcony. Once again, my plans were foiled.

The phone rang. I downed my drink in one gulp and snatched up the receiver. "Yes?" I wasn't even polite. My grandmothers would have had a fit!

"Hey, girl!" It was Glory. "Ronnie's down here and we've been talking."

"What?! Walker's here again?"

"Yeah. We need to come up and see you…right now. Sally's supposed to take over in ten minutes, but she's here already and said she'd watch the desk."

I sighed. "Okay…" and hung up. I was exhausted, but very curious. What was this about? I glanced down at my outfit and decided the heck with it. If they don't like flannel, tough. I'm not changing!

I looked around the loft. Still a mess, but I just couldn't face the finger print powder. I suppose I'll hire someone to come in and clean—once this case is over.

I started a fire since I was going to be up all night…again… and contemplated serving hot chocolate. Or maybe cognac. I didn't know their agenda, so I postponed making that decision.

They arrived and Ronnie walked in, surveying the place. Some nerve!

I took Glory off to the side and said, "So…you're on a first name basis with this character?"

She tried to look sheepish. Didn't succeed. "Just hear him out, Kate." She nudged me with her elbow "…Isn't he just the cutest thing?" she said, looking him over.

Mental eye roll.

"Nice place you've got here," commented Ronnie. "And I like what you've done with the dust in your office."

That pissed me off! "You oughtta know…," I started.

Glory cut in, "Now, you two. Let's just sit and Ronnie, you can tell Kate what's on your mind."

I took a deep breath and counted to ten. Then I did it again. I reached *way* down deep inside myself and pulled out some manners.

They headed for the couch in front of the fire and I inquired about drinks. They both opted for gin and tonics and I poured myself an XO. I needed something stronger than bourbon!

I curled up in a chair by the cozy fire and listened to Ronnie. It was late when he finished, but we were all wide awake. He'd come up with a cool plan of attack!

CHAPTER 53

Lieutenant Whitaker

———— ● ————

Monday Evening

"...**a**nd I guess when Marlow checked out the warehouse, he just found one of the workmen who'd been hanging out there," Whitaker told Carlos. "Ended up just taking the guy home."

"Amazing!" Carlos commented. "Kate was sure that was the hiding place...guess she was wrong on this one, huh?"

"It happens."

"Where are you and Stevens headed now?"

"We just heard from Unit 276, staked out at Pasta Mama's. Looks like Walker's been inside for about twenty minutes and Mancini just arrived...is headed in, too. We're on our way over there. You still at the station?"

"Right now I am," replied Whitaker, "but I'm going over to the Bryant house in a few minutes."

"Got it...we'll let you know how this scene goes down...426 over."

It bugged Whitaker when someone questioned Kate's talents. He'd been really surprised when the warehouse had been clean. Kate had been so excited and so sure this was the place. He didn't like it when she was disappointed. But he was also angry with himself. *Thoughts like these aren't going to solve anything...especially this case. Get on with it, man!* Lieutenant Whitaker leaned back in his chair and rested his feet on the desk. He needed to think. *I wonder if there's a chance that Marlow missed something when he checked out the warehouse,* he thought.

CHAPTER 54

Emerson

———●———

Early Monday Evening

Where is everyone? And what the hell's going on? Emerson drove past the warehouse on Monroe Street three more times before he felt it was safe to stop.

This afternoon, late, he'd been going to move Eddie to another hiding place. He'd waited half an hour too long. When he'd come to get Joey and the boy, two cop cars had been there! The side door had been wide open. The first car had been empty—cops must've been inside. The second car had just pulled in and there were two officers still sitting there.

Emerson had waited on a side street for what seemed like an eternity and then made another pass by the building. Door was closed…cop cars gone. After another little while, he'd swung past again. No sign of anyone.

Finally he got up his nerve. He pulled into another lot two buildings down. He didn't think he'd been tailed. After looking up and down the street for a few minutes, he made his way to the building, key in hand. He had a story made up in case he was stopped. But he wasn't.

He entered the side door and let his eyes adjust. "Joey!" he called out. He listened for a reply. No answer.

He stuck his head in the office. They had cleaned up all the trash just like they'd been told. Good. But the sleeping bag was still there. *Hmmm.* He began walking towards the cafeteria. He was almost there when something in his peripheral vision caught his attention.

A whole tower of boxes had toppled over and were scattered around the aisle. There were pop cans and other trash as well. It looked like the stuff he'd told Joey and Eddie to clean up from the office. Emerson looked around and could imagine the scenario.

Eddie'd skipped out. But where was Joey? And if the cops knew anything about Eddie, why weren't they crawling all over this place?

Suddenly, Emerson got very nervous. He was afraid this whole thing was a setup. Cops were probably everywhere...spying on him and on this building. He panicked! He needed to get out of here—fast!

He rushed back to the side door. Just before he blasted through it, he came to his senses. He stopped and got a grip on his paranoia. "You can't go barreling out of here," he chided himself. "You'll give yourself away. You got to be cool...nonchalant...take it easy."

He allowed himself a few seconds to calm down, then walked outside, turned and locked the door. Then he walked down the street whistling a tune. He kept his hands in his trouser pockets, however, because they were still shaking.

CHAPTER 55

Eddie

Monday Night

Eddie's head snapped up and he was instantly alert. Had a noise awakened him? Or was it his dream? He'd been talking to Joey. The dream was hazy, but he remembered that much. Joey. He still felt bad about him. Then Eddie remembered what they'd talked about. Because he'd escaped from the warehouse, Joey wasn't going to get paid. The thought made Eddie feel even worse.

Eddie clenched his teeth to keep them from chattering. He needed to listen. If he *had* heard a noise, it was gone now. He didn't know how long he'd been asleep, but he felt around where he was sitting. The ground under his bottom was cold and there was a little dew on the grass. He'd watched enough movies to know about these things. He'd been there a while. It wasn't even beginning to get light, however, so he figured it was still the middle of the night. He snuggled deeper into his sweatshirt, but it was no use. He needed to find somewhere to spend the rest of the night.

Eddie considered his alternatives. He really should go to the cops. But he didn't know how to get to them. He could call them, but he didn't have a phone. There was probably a pay phone somewhere, but he was afraid to come out of hiding. Uncle Emerson might find him. If he could find a phone, he could call home, but if Uncle Emerson was in on this, maybe his parents were, too! *They may all be plotting against me!* he thought unhappily.

Eddie tried to remember. What had he done to get himself in this much trouble? Maybe it was the parent conference his parents had attended last week. It was the first one of the year, but this teacher had said the same thing as every other teacher he'd ever had. Eddie was a "dreamer" with "a lot of brains and not much ambition". Blah, blah, blah. Every year, the same old story. Eddie thought a little longer and then made a silent pact with God: "Get me out of this, and I promise I'll work harder."

Eddie shivered again. He could take a chance with whoever lived in this house. "Nah," he whispered softly. "They'd make me call home." So much for his options.

While it was still daylight he'd noticed a garage and some other buildings near the house where he was hiding. Maybe one would be unlocked and he could sneak inside. No one seemed to be out at this hour and the house was dark, so he stealthily crossed the vast yard, going from tree to tree.

Heart pounding, he tried the first door. The garage was locked. Rats! But there was a pool house and its door was open. Eddie slipped silently inside. He didn't want to turn on any lights, so felt his way around. Pool vacuum, hose, skimmer, chemicals. Refrigerator. His stomach rumbled. He was so hungry! But he was afraid to open it in case the light would come on and attract someone's attention. He felt around some more and found a door leading to a small bathroom. He went inside and relieved his bladder. That helped, but he was still hungry. Instead of worrying about food, he gulped volumes of water from the sink to fill his stomach. Feeling a bit better, he resumed his search. Eventually he found a cupboard…with towels inside. Perfect!

Eddie made a nest with some of the towels. He could fit in the cupboard if he scrunched in real tight, so he climbed in, covered up with two more towels, pulled the door almost closed and was asleep again in no time.

CHAPTER 56

Westminster Terrace

⬥

Earlier Monday Night

"Oh, Jeeze...look who's here," Emerson said as he turned onto Westminster. He realized that he'd begun to sweat and his hands were trembling again. "This ought to be interesting."

As he pulled up to Arlington's house, his fears were confirmed: there sat the lieutenant's car. He was tempted to drive on, but then he reconsidered. He parked, willed himself back into his carefree mode and walked to the door. He entered and found the group of people standing in the kitchen.

"Hi, Em," Penn Allister greeted him. We're just making some tea before we go back to the library. Shall I get a cup for you?"

"No, thanks. I'm not staying long...just came to see if you've heard anything."

"The water's hot...let's go into the other room." Penn Allister carried the teapot and Arlington had a tray with cups, saucers, sugar and spoons. Lieutenant Whitaker and Emerson followed, empty-handed.

"Oh, Emerson, grab the little pitcher of milk that's in the fridge, will you?" Penn Allister called over her shoulder. "Someone might like some milk in their tea."

Emerson returned from the kitchen as the parade was making its way through the foyer. The front door opened and Kate Jeffers burst in.

"Doug...you've got to come..." she began. Jeffers' words died on her lips as she noticed Emerson coming out of the kitchen.

Whitaker started to reply, but caught the look on Kate's face. Something was up! But she obviously didn't want to talk in front of the family. "Why don't you join us in the library, Kate? Then I'd like to talk with you privately, if the Bryants don't mind."

"Sure..." She plastered a smile on her face and followed.

Was that a look of gratitude that she had shot in his direction?

As soon as was polite, Whitaker excused himself and Jeffers. Electricity shot up his arm when she grabbed it and pulled him aside. He made himself focus on the information she was telling him and followed her outside. Sure enough, there sat Gloria and Ronnie in Kate's car. *Are they making out in there?* he asked himself. Ronnie, supposedly, had decided to work with them on this case.

Whitaker wondered, on the short drive back to the station, what had happened to change Walker's mind.

CHAPTER 57

Emerson at Westminster Terrace

———— ● ————

Earlier Monday Night

Emerson Bryant didn't think things could get much worse. Eddie and Joey had disappeared. The warehouse was totally empty. It looked as though there'd been some sort of scuffle there. Boxes had been scattered on the warehouse floor. And the cops had been sniffing around.

But things had looked surprisingly quiet here at the house when he'd arrived a while earlier. Just the usual police scene—not the flurry of activity he'd have expected. He had decided to go in and find out what they knew.

When he had first walked into the house, he'd heard voices in the kitchen. The maid had *surely* gone home by now—must be the family. He'd followed the sound. Arlington and Lieutenant Whitaker had merely nodded to him. Penn had spoken and seemed happy he was there. Nothing seemed unusual. Huh! *So far, so good,* he'd thought.

When they had been returning to the library, Penn Allister asked him to get the milk for the tea. Emerson didn't mind doing that—there wouldn't be enough time for them to plan any surprises behind his back. But when he'd come back out of the kitchen, the Jeffers woman was coming in the front door! She had looked excited about something. *Shit!* Did she know something? Was she going to blow things for him?

Emerson had swallowed the bile that had risen in his throat. *Calm down. Just one thing at a time,* he'd told himself. *Just sit tight and see what happens.*

Jeffers had stopped mid-sentence. She'd given the lieutenant a "look". Then she had joined the family in the library looking calm as anything. *Why the change?* He'd wondered. Emerson had listened carefully and snuck glances at Kate Jeffers. The more he searched her face, the more he realized that she looked about to pop. *What's going on?* he'd asked himself again. *Maybe she had another one of her "visions".* Emerson snickered.

They had started talking about the warehouse: "...We had officers check out the buildings. They only found one that looked at all suspicious, but even *that* didn't pan out for us," the lieutenant told them.

So, Emerson had thought smugly, *"they still don't know shit!"* He'd begun to feel a little better, but found it impossible to sit still. He'd helped himself to the bourbon and downed a shot—that should help him relax. He'd poured a second drink and had gone back to his seat.

A short while later Jeffers and the lieutenant had risen from their seats and excused themselves for a private talk. Emerson's skin had prickled. He wished he could do *something* to keep Jeffers from telling Whitaker any news. But the bourbon was taking effect and he felt rooted to his chair. He rationalized. Chances are he was over-reacting. She probably didn't know any more than the rest of them.

CHAPTER 58

Kate, Glory and Ronnie

———— ● ————

Earlier Monday Night

I had phoned Lieutenant Whitaker's private line in his office. No answer. When I tried the front desk, they said he'd gone to the Bryants' on Westminster Terrace. I really didn't want to show up there with Glory and Ronnie in tow, but I didn't have much choice, did I?

There were lives at stake here, and the sooner Ronnie got to talk with Doug Whitaker, the better. *If* what Lou had told him was true, then Ronnie was in grave danger too. So what better place to come than here—a house full of cops!

Our unlikely group pulled up in front of the house next door— too many cars parked out in front of the Bryants'.

"You guys stay here until I talk with Doug," I had told Gloria and Ronnie.

Glory started to pout, but then I guess she began to think about all the advantages of being *alone* in the back seat of my car with Ronnie.

Oh, brother! I did another mental eye roll.

"Hey, Kate, wait," Ronnie had said excitedly, grabbing my arm. "That might be Emerson's car up there. His looks sort of like that...I can't see that well. We'll be fine here. And believe me, there's no way I want to go inside that house—*I* was the one that Arlington paid off five years ago. He might remember."

I cautioned them to keep their eyes on the neighborhood in case Lou or one of his cronies had followed us. Then I ran up the steps.

The light was on in the foyer and I could see Penn Allister heading my way, her hands full. I waved to her through the glass door and let myself in. Doug was behind her, as was the rest of the family.

I started to tell Whitaker that Ronnie was sitting in my car when Emerson suddenly appeared from the back of the house. I choked on my words! Luckily, Whitaker must have seen the look on my face because he covered for me. I followed the group into the library and calmly (yeah, right!) took a cup of tea.

On the inside, I was a basket-case! I could feel Emerson Bryant's eyes boring into me and it was all I could do to keep it together. I heard almost nothing that was said and I'm sure I looked visibly relieved when Doug finally requested a private chat with me.

I practically *dragged* him back into the foyer and told him about my passengers. Then I raced outside to make sure they were still there and were safe.

Whitaker followed—at a more sedate pace, but I could tell that *he* was excited, too.

We conferred on the front porch for a moment and concluded that the station was the best place for our talk with Ronnie. Whitaker led the way and we followed in my car.

———◆◆◆◆———

The four of us talked for *hours*. When Ronnie'd finished his statement and we'd worked out a plan for Tuesday, the three of us headed back to my place. I left Glory and Ronnie in the garage and took the elevator upstairs. I needed sleep!

"Hi," said a familiar voice—the one with a Greek accent! "I wondered if you'd *ever* get home."

Papa was leaning on the door to my loft. Instantly, my heart started doing its little pitty-pat thing and I got a warm feeling—all over. I was afraid I might pass out! I don't think it was from lack of sleep, however, since we managed to stay up for a couple more hours before finally crashing.

CHAPTER 59

Eddie

———————●———————

Tuesday Morning

Eddie woke up. It took him a second to remember where he was. Then he pushed the cabinet door open and peeked out. Sunlight was streaming through the window. How long had he slept?

He crawled out of the cupboard and stretched his legs. He was small, but even so, he'd had to curl up all night and his legs were cramping. Man, would he like to jump in these people's pool and relax for a while…Steam was rising, so it was obviously heated.

"Yeah, right," he admonished himself. "Like that's going to happen!"

His stomach rumbled, reminding him how long it had been since he'd eaten and he looked longingly at the little refrigerator in the pool house. He knew it was wrong to steal, but he opened it anyway. There were cans of soda and some apples. He took one of each.

Now what? he asked himself when he'd finished eating. He folded up all the towels and used the bathroom. After making certain to leave everything just as he'd found it, he grabbed one more apple and stuffed it in his pocket along with the empty pop can and apple core. He crept out into the yard.

Seeing no one, he made his way from tree to tree, back to the bushes next to the street. He knelt there for a few minutes, deciding where to go.

Whom could he trust? He came up with two possibilities: his sister, Janie and probably the cops.

He pulled the hood of his sweatshirt up to hide his face. Even though it was sunny, the air had a nip to it, so no one would think it odd to see him dressed like this.

He stepped out of the bushes onto Ponce De Leon and started walking back the way he had come. As he walked, he tried to remember what they'd passed Friday afternoon on their way to the warehouse. He remembered seeing just one corner of Piedmont Park as they'd driven down Monroe. The park might be a good place to hide out for a while. And the other side of the park wasn't too far from his house. If he could cut across…he might be able to find Janie without anyone else knowing he was there.

"Ha! I've got a plan," he said aloud, congratulating himself. He suddenly felt better than he had for a long time. He crossed Monroe and turned right. North. He could tell by the sun. Lucky he'd been paying attention in science class the day they'd discussed that. And *they* said he was a dreamer! Hah!

He passed the row of warehouses, glad that he was on the opposite side of the street. The lots were filled with cars, but none that he recognized. He wondered if he should go over to see if Joey was at work, but just the thought of going back in that building gave him the willies. He kept walking.

Soon he could see the park entrance in the distance. But across the street, a block closer, was a police station! He hadn't remembered that it was there. *Now what?!* he asked himself. Should he stick with his plan of finding Janie or go to the police?

CHAPTER 60

Emerson

———————⬤———————

Tuesday Morning

Emerson's brain felt fuzzy. He'd had a few drinks at Arlington and Penn Allister's the night before. Even though he'd been a little buzzed, he'd driven around the area for a couple of hours looking for Eddie. When he couldn't find him anywhere, he remembered about Joey. *Christ! Why didn't you think of him before?* he admonished himself.

He had knocked at Joey's door and roused him from his bed. Joey appeared to have been sound asleep—unconcerned about what was happening with Emerson and Eddie.

Exasperated with the slow man, he'd said, "Man, I've been going crazy looking for you and Eddie—and here you are…asleep!"

"Sorry, Mr. Bryant," Joey had replied, looking down and shuffling his feet. "I was tired."

"Let me in and tell me what the hell happened. I drove up and there were cops everywhere!"

Joey stood to one side and let Emerson into his tiny living room. They sat down and Joey told his side of the story to Emerson.

"The cop brought you *home?*" he'd asked incredulously when Joey'd finished.

"Yeah...I didn't say anything about Eddie. I didn't know where he'd gone and I didn't want to get in trouble."

"Jesus Maria," Emerson had said and then thought to himself, *I guess Joey's smarter than I thought!* "Well, go back to bed, man. There's nothing else for you to do. And be sure to go to work today. You don't want anyone to suspect anything."

Emerson had gotten back in his car thinking that what he'd heard was true: no one knew anything about Eddie and the cops didn't suspect Joey. *What a bunch of losers!*

Even so...he needed to be careful. He'd driven around a little longer, until he felt like he was going to fall asleep at the wheel. Then he went back to his place to crash for a couple hours before taking up the hunt for Eddie again. Maybe this time he'd be so tired that he wouldn't have the nightmare.

⬤━❊━⬤

Later Tuesday morning he continued his search. He drove past the warehouses and past the park. He went up and down the surrounding streets, but saw no sign of the boy.

"Well," said Emerson aloud. "I guess it doesn't really matter. I'll get the money tonight even if I *don't* find him. I'll deal with the rest of it later. So what if Eddie doesn't show. This is all Arlington's fault anyway."

But he kept on looking.

CHAPTER 61

Kate

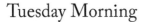

Tuesday Morning

My alarm went off at 6:00. Ugh! Less than three hours of sleep. My head felt like dog meat...But there were *other* parts of my body that hadn't felt this good for months!

I looked to my left. Papa was still here. I felt a tingly sensation...I considered seriously about waking him up and continuing where we'd left off the night before. No, wait. That was only a couple of hours ago. I decided against it: a girl can take only so much at one time.

I staggered into my robe and stumbled to the coffee machine. *G-rrr.* I had forgotten to program the thing last night. I started a pot and leaned against the counter. I think I fell back to sleep for the ten minutes it took to brew. But the smell of coffee is for me, like the sirens calling Odysseus. Okay...maybe it was just the gurgling of the machine as it completed its task that woke me up. At any rate, I poured myself a very large mug and tip-toed back upstairs to the shower.

While the water was warming up I snuck a long look at Papa. He looked so good, lying there, his hair all rumpled. Was that a slight smile I noticed on his face?

Half an hour later I poured another mug—to go—and wrote what I hoped was a sexy, witty note to Papa. I left it next to the coffee machine where he'd be sure to see it. Then I headed to the station.

<hr />

Doug Whitaker was already there when I arrived. Did the guy *never* go home? Then I remembered about his wife dying a few years back. How awful! I started daydreaming about Papa. What would it be like to be married to him and then have something happen to him? To go home to an empty house and know he wouldn't be there—ever again. That I'd never lay eyes on him again. I broke into tears right there in the middle of the station.

"Kate…Are you okay?" Whitaker asked.

I snapped back to the present and shook my head a couple of times. "Yeah, I'm fine," I squeaked. I blinked my eyes a few times and cleared my throat. "Just a little tired, that's all."

"I know. We all are. Come on back to the conference room. The detectives are already here. You can help me update Williams and Stevens."

I fished in my pocket, found a partially unused tissue and honked my nose as I followed the lieutenant down the hall.

I stuffed the tissue back into my bag and my hand bumped up against my cell phone. I tugged it out and noticed that my sister, Emily, had left me a voice mail late last night. She was still on the top of my to-do list.

<hr />

We'd just finished filling Amy and Carlos in on last night's events when the most bizarre thing happened.

The sergeant who was manning the front desk came back to the conference room with a little kid…who was wearing a green sweatshirt!

"Sir," he said, directing himself to Whitaker. "I've got someone who'd like to talk with you—all of you."

"Holy Moly!" Carlos murmured.

CHAPTER 62

Arlington

●

Tuesday Morning

The offices of Arlington Bryant's law firm were on the top floor of a mid-rise building in downtown Atlanta. He stood at his window on the fifteenth floor, taking in the view. "Just last Friday I was standing here enjoying this," he said to no one in particular. "Now—four days later—I wonder if I'll ever love this city again."

"Mr. Bryant..." his speaker phone crackled. "There's a Doug Whitaker on line two. Can you take the call?"

Arlington excitedly turned toward his desk. "Yes, I'll pick up. Thanks." His heart began to hammer.

———— ⬥ ————

Arlington put down the receiver. No wonder the lieutenant had called him at the office. There would be no way he could have taken that call at home!

He grabbed his suit coat and hurried out of his office. "Sorry, Toni," Bryant said to his receptionist. "I hate to ask you to do this, but you're going to have to cancel the rest of my meetings and conference calls today. Something's come up. You can reach me on my cell if there's an emergency, but *only you*. Don't let anyone else know where I can be reached. I need the line to stay open."

"Okay, sir," a very confused and curious Toni answered as she watched her employer hurry out the door. "I wonder what *that's* all about," she murmured.

———◆※◆———

Arlington Bryant sped to the Monroe Street Police Station. He screeched to a halt in front of the building. Without bothering to turn off the ignition, he bounded from his car, blasted through the doors and down the hall to the conference room.

"Eddie! Eddie…" He grabbed the boy into his arms and smothered him with hugs and kisses. "Oh my God," he kept repeating.

He held Eddie (who was crying, but grinning as well) at arm's length as though he couldn't believe his eyes. "You're all right? Are you sure?" Then he squashed Eddie against his chest again, holding him tight.

"Da-a-ad," Eddie whined. "I can't breathe!"

Arlington loosened his death-grip on his son, not knowing whether to laugh or cry.

"Your keys, Mr. Bryant." The desk sergeant said, coming in the door. He ended up handing the set to Whitaker since Arlington was unaware of anyone in the room except Eddie. The sergeant smiled, pleased that at least *one* case was going to have a happy ending.

After father and son had been reunited, Detectives Williams and Stevens and Kate Jeffers joined the other three in the conference room.

"We are thrilled your son is safe, Mr. Bryant," Whitaker began. "Now what we'd like you to do is keep this whole thing under wraps and help us take down the people who did this. I realize it is *completely* unfair to ask you to keep this from your wife and the rest of your family, but I'm going to ask for your cooperation anyway."

"Not tell Penn Allister?" Arlington asked incredulously. He breathed in deeply and exhaled slowly, considering the fall-out from that move.

Lieutenant Whitaker and the others filled Arlington and Eddie Bryant in on the plan.

CHAPTER 63

Kate

●

Tuesday Afternoon

I finally had a little down time, so I grabbed my phone and headed out to my rooftop garden. I cringed when I noticed my wilted flowers and mentally added another chore to my 'to do' list.

The morning had started out blustery, but the wind had died down during the day and the afternoon sun felt warm on my face. I'd gotten the call from Whitaker late morning, saying Eddie Bryant was safe and sound and I'd been feeling great ever since. The feeling of doom had been lifted. True, we were going to go ahead with the ransom drop later in the evening, in hopes of catching the kidnapper. And I knew all too well that an operation such as Whitaker had designed was risky. But it would be worth trying in order to get to the bottom of the kidnapping. Arlington Bryant and Eddie were being real troopers about all this. I'm sure Eddie wanted nothing more than to go home and see his mother and sister and to get his life back to normal. But instead, he and his dad were deep in hiding for the remainder of the day. And I was getting excited about the prospect of closure on this case. I was feeling good. But as I sat on my patio, a feeling of unease crept over me again.

I closed my eyes and tried to get in touch with the niggling feeling. This was a different sensation than I'd ever felt before. *Is this another aspect of my psychic abilities?* I wondered. I tried to open myself up to the feeling. There was some sort of power struggle going on. I explored the Eddie Bryant case. But it didn't feel right. As I sat, the feeling got stronger. This struggle was physical, not mental. As though someone was literally trying to overpower another person. I sensed a man and woman.

The sensation passed. I was still troubled by the feelings, but couldn't pick up any more vibes. Frustrated, I glanced at my cell and decided that I'm better return Emily's call before having to meet Whitaker for the ransom drop.

My sister picked up on the first ring and the feelings of a struggle hit me right between the eyes.

"Emily, what's wrong?" I asked the second I heard her voice.

"I need to talk to you," she said, her voice barely a whisper. "Can I come over?"

I paced the floor, frantic, during the twenty minutes it took her to get to my loft. Finally I took the elevator to the parking garage and met her as she pulled in. My heart stopped when I saw her emerge from her car. She looked disheveled. Her eyes were sunken and there were deep, dark circles under them as though she hadn't seen sleep for days. She looked pale and much thinner than when I'd last seen her. She staggered a bit as she came forward and I rushed to her side, putting my arm around her waist for support. Tears slipped from her eyes as we made our way back to the elevator and upstairs.

Once inside, I guided her to the sofa where she immediately curled up under a chenille throw. She shivered in spite of the warm sun pouring through the windows.

I dashed to the kitchen to brew some tea, hesitant to leave her side for even a minute. While the water heated I gathered my thoughts and courage and approached the sofa.

"Hell's fire, Emily. What in God's name has happened?"

She smiled tentatively from under the blanket. "I've had a rough couple 'o' weeks."

I waited silently and watched as she struggled, deciding what to tell me.

"I thought I'd be all right, you know? But I'm not. You know the guy I was seeing? Ian. The one I broke up with a couple months ago?"

I nodded, my sense of unease getting stronger by the second.

"Well, he had a problem with it. So he started following me and calling me saying all this awful stuff. I pretty much told him to get lost and tried to ignore him. When his number came up on my caller ID, I wouldn't answer. I'd shut off my phone and then he'd stop for a couple days. But it felt like he was always right behind me. I thought about getting a restraining order against him, but he never came that close. And then, when I started going out with Nate—oh, do you know about him?"

I nodded. "Sarah said something about a new man in your life. Is Nate his name?"

Her head bobbed up and down and I noticed another hint of a smile, but it faded quickly. "He's really sweet. Anyway, when Ian realized that I was seeing someone else, he lost it. A couple weeks ago when I got back to my room, he was waiting for me."

My palms were sweating as I tried to remain calm and give her time to continue. I wiped them on my pants. Emily looked so pitiful. I wanted to find this Ian—and kill him with my bare hands! "Your teakettle is boiling, Kate," Emily announced.

Exasperated, I turned from the sofa and ran back to the kitchen. I suppose it was good to give Emily time to compose herself before telling me the rest, but I was dying inside. I managed to get our tea back to the sofa without dumping it and hurried back to the kitchen for the milk and sugar that I knew she'd want. I kept my eyes on her the entire time.

Emily sat up, calmly prepared her drink, and took a few sips before continuing. "He jumped out of nowhere just as I stuck my key in the door. He threw me up against the wall. I cracked my head. It made me dizzy, but I could hear him ranting…" Her voice trailed off.

I watched as Emily then completely closed in on herself. I've never seen anything like it. She was practically catatonic. She sat perfectly still for the longest time. Her eyes remained unfocused, but I knew she was remembering that night. I wasn't sure what to do. *Should I wait quietly or perhaps say something?* I wrestled with myself. Finally, I just reached out and softly touched her arm. It broke her trance.

"Oh," she whispered. "You know, I don't think I want to talk about this anymore. I thought I remembered everything, but I don't. Maybe I'll be able to tell you more later."

I freaked out! "Emily!" I tried not to raise my voice. "You don't remember what happened? Think…try to tell me."

She shook her head. "I guess I blacked out. I remember waking up and I was on the floor. No one else was there. It was dark out. So I guess I'd been there a while. My head still hurt, so I went to bed."

"That's all? You don't remember anything else? What about Ian? Did he hurt you?"

Emily shrugged as she looked at me for a while. Then her eyes slid over towards the French doors and she looked out at the bright autumn afternoon. "I don't remember, Kate. I thought talking to you might help me recall what happened, but it doesn't. I'm really tired. Can I take a nap here on the sofa?" she asked as she put her tea down and burrowed under the blanket.

❖

I hated to leave Emily. But Lieutenant Whitaker was counting on me to help with the ransom drop. I couldn't let him and the others down. I was torn between my loyalty to my family and my job.

But Emily said she understood the situation and that I had to go. She assured me that she was sleepy and would be right there on the sofa when I got home. She seemed completely rational.

As I gathered my things to go, I could hear her soft, steady breathing. I tip-toed around the loft and turned on a couple lamps in case Emily woke up before I returned.

I was ready to leave when Emily suddenly screamed and sat upright on the sofa. I raced back to her, noting the terrified look in her eyes. Putting my arms around her, I rocked her back and forth, murmuring nonsense.

"Promise me you'll be back, Kate," she whimpered. "Promise me you won't get hurt. I can't lose you, too."

I smoothed her hair and got her settled back under the throw. I couldn't bring myself to promise anything. Not after our parents' deaths. One never knows what will happen. Instead I assured her that I'd try to be back as soon as possible...and I'd bring Chinese. She smiled at that.

I waited until she was asleep again and then made my way down to the parking garage to wait for Whitaker.

CHAPTER 64

Carlos & Amy

———— ● ————

Late Tuesday Afternoon

Detectives Williams and Stevens, in their unmarked car, had been sitting in the garage at Hartsfield for an hour. They'd watched as all the parties had assembled.

Ronnie Walker was first. He'd exited his vehicle, the same beat-up Chrysler, and entered the terminal.

Lieutenant Whitaker and Kate Jeffers arrived next. Kate got out of Whitaker's vehicle, stretched, and surveyed the parking lot.

Then Lou Mancini pulled up and parked near the terminal entrance. "I didn't know *he* was part of the equation," commented Amy. "This could be a problem. We'd better get on the radio and make sure Whitaker knows he's here."

Finally the EMT crew arrived and lay back near the entrance ramp.

The detectives didn't pay close attention to the other cars in the parking garage. There were two other cars they should have noticed. One was one black sedan with deeply tinted windows.

The man inside was watching Lou Mancini carefully, his semi-automatic loaded and waiting on the seat next to him. The second vehicle was an old van which Glory had converted into her home away from home.

"What the…" exclaimed Carlos, straining forward in his seat to get a better view. "Amy—look…check this out!"

"It's a black walrus?"

"Walruses are not black."

Amy leaned toward Carlos and squinted through the windshield. "It's wiggling between the cars. Where's it going, Carlos? What the heck is it?"

"I think it's a woman. Sure is a big one. Keep your eye on her, Amy, and I'll radio Whitaker again. Man, this place is turning into a circus!"

They watched as Kate retrieved a heavy suitcase from the rear of Whitaker's vehicle and wrestled it to an upright position. She pulled up the handle, nodded to Doug, and wheeled the bag toward the terminal doors.

Amy tapped Carlos on the arm and motioned in Kate's direction. "There she goes. Let's move. We've got to keep her in our sights."

"I've always thought it ironic," commented Carlos as he and Amy hustled toward the building, "that it's called a terminal. I thought 'terminal' meant 'fatal'.

"That's not funny. I hate it when you try to be cute!"

CHAPTER 65

Whitaker Tuesday Evening

———————●———————

K ate rode to Hartsfield International with Doug Whitaker. The lieutenant knew that the kidnappers wanted Kate to be the one to take the money to Terminal F, and he didn't like it. She no longer carried a weapon; she'd be a sitting duck. And she wasn't her usual self. She seemed distracted. The operation could be doomed if any one of the players wasn't in top form. And he had feelings for her—even if he couldn't admit it—protective feelings—not in the paternal sense, either.

"Damn it, keep your mind on your job," he grumbled at himself.

"What?" Kate, lost in her own thoughts, turned to look at him. "Did you say something?"

Instantly, Whitaker blushed and his palms began to sweat. "Nah…nothing."

Kate pulled her mind from Emily's troubles and tried to focus on the evening's mission. "Don't you like the plan? I mean, what can possibly go wrong?"

Whitaker grimaced. "Don't say that…you'll jinx the operation… and yes, I have misgivings—this whole thing could backfire…" His voice trailed off and he wiped his hands on the legs of his pants. He'd lost his wife of ten years when she'd inadvertently gotten in the middle of a sting. He shuddered at the memory. That had been four years ago. He didn't want to lose someone else—especially Kate.

"Here we are," he said, glad to have the trip behind him. He moved to the right-hand lane and exited the freeway. Just a couple more minutes and he could focus on something other than the woman sitting next to him. *Man, what a distraction!* he thought.

They traveled up the ramp to the top floor. The detectives were already in place. But Whitaker didn't acknowledge them, just in case... He pulled to his designated position.

"Don't worry, Doug. I'll be careful. I'll have Ronnie with me and Amy and Carlos will be there as well," Kate said as she began gathering her things together to make it into Terminal F.

"Kate," Whitaker began. Their eyes locked, briefly, and his mouth went dry. "Be careful," he croaked. He cleared he throat and added, "I'll be in radio contact with you all the way. Come back safe."

"Sure thing." Kate got out of the car and stretched. "I'll wait out here for a minute before I go in. Let's test my wire while we wait."

That job finished, Kate hauled the ransom bag out of the back seat. "Jesus, Doug, this thing's heavy," she complained, grunting. She pulled up the handle, nodded to Whitaker, and rolled the bag to the terminal doors.

Whitaker took a deep breath and breathed out slowly.

"Lieutenant...this is 426...we've got an unusual situation here. There is a female subject crawling between the cars here on the departure level. We need to follow Kate, so someone else will need to check out this woman. 426...out."

The Lieutenant watched as his two detectives followed Kate at a distance and disappeared inside. Then he saw Glory. *Oh, my God!* he said to himself.

CHAPTER 66

Glory

___●___

Tuesday Evening

Glory wasn't about to sit on her backside and let this action take place without her! She had several reasons to get to the airport…She needed to prove to Kate that she would make a kick-ass partner. She needed to show Ronnie that she could be counted on to help out when he needed her…"And," she said as she hopped in her van, "he is going to need me tonight!"

She had a feeling about this—she wasn't real comfortable with the plan—she was afraid something would go wrong. And she wanted, no…*needed* to be there if it did.

She headed South on Interstate 75, towards Hartsfield. *Damn good thing I was able to switch shifts with Sally,* thought Glory. Sally'd been a real gem to do two shifts, back-to-back. One was boring enough. Gloria made a mental note that she owed Sally a big one!

She wound around the access road and finally pulled into the parking structure at Terminal F. Gloria glanced at her clock.

Five-thirty. Good…just in time. She parked where she could see Ronnie's car.

Here came Kate and Lieutenant Whitaker. Glory scrunched down in her seat. She didn't want them to see her. They'd be pissed! They pulled into a parking space close to the terminal entrance.

Suddenly, she noticed a familiar face—at least she thought so. There was a man, sitting in a vehicle just watching the people walking by. She didn't have a real clear view, but it sure looked like Lou, Ronnie's boss. Ronnie'd shown her a picture earlier. Was that really the same guy? *He* wasn't supposed to be here! *He* was supposed be waiting back at the club.

"Uh-oh," Glory said. "I'd better check this guy out. But this needs to be a *covert* operation," she continued, aloud. "Good thing I changed into my surveillance outfit—everything black, from my combat boots to my spandex top. Hell, I even wore my black lace undies!"

Very quietly, she opened her door and slithered to the pavement. She pushed the door of her van closed with her shoulder until she heard it click. She didn't want to run the battery down by leaving the interior light on—she might need to make a speedy get-away.

Dropping to her hands and knees, she made her way among the parked cars, occasionally checking over her shoulder to make certain she wasn't being followed.

When she was finally in a good position to see that it was, indeed, Lou, she flattened herself as much as possible and crabbed sideways under a vehicle.

"Thank God for high-profile SUVs," she muttered. "If this was a damned 'vette, I wouldn't stand a chance!"

CHAPTER 67

Lou

---⬤---

Tuesday Evening

Lou Mancini sat in his car in the parking structure at Hartsfield Airport. He watched the entrance to the International Terminal and let his thoughts wander…It was all supposed to go down tonight. Finally, he'd get his money. He'd been carrying this Bryant loser for too long! He'd felt sorry for him—out of work again.

Lou shook his head, disgusted with himself. Getting soft in his old age. How stupid was that? You can't feel sorry for anyone and be in the business that he was in! Feelings—they suck! And can get you into a whole pile of trouble.

Look where having feelings about Ronnie had gotten him. He'd been like a big brother – no, like a *dad* to the kid for years. And now the scumbag was following his dick instead of using his brain. Has the hots for some chick and is turning against Lou. He's going to try to go straight—Lou could feel it! He could see right through Ronnie. He'd always been a lousy liar.

Lou allowed his thoughts drift back to when Ronnie'd been fifteen. He'd been living with Lou for three or four years by then. He'd stayed at the house while Lou'd gone back to the club for a few hours.

Lou had gone downstairs to talk to the on-duty manager for a few minutes. When he'd gotten back to the office there'd been a message on the answering machine. It was from Ronnie: "Lou, it's me. I'm really tired, so I'm headed to bed. Don't bother to call—I won't hear the phone. I'll see ya in the morning. G'night."

Yeah, right! Lou'd laughed out loud at *that* one! Going to bed—at ten o'clock. That'll be the day. Ronnie never crashed till one or two. He was up to something—that was a "given".

Lou'd quickly finished up at the office and run down the back stairs to his car. That had been back in the day…before his accident. Lou could barely walk, now!

Lou had turned into the alley behind the house that he and Ronnie shared just in time to see his old Cavalier pulling out onto the street ahead. Lou'd followed. Ronnie *had* to be the driver.

Lou himself had taught the kid to drive, out on the back roads in Gwinnett County. But at fifteen, Ronnie hadn't even gotten his *permit* yet, let alone his license! Lou had been meaning to take him to get his permit for several weeks—but he'd just been too busy—the club, Prosciutto's, was really starting to do well—but there were a lot of management issues.

Lou had followed Ronnie; he was headed to a friend's house—some guy he'd met at school.

Yeah, Lou had made sure Ron went to school every day—the kid was smart—maybe he'd be able to take over the club one day. Lou'd even left it to him in his will. He'd have to remember to change that, after all this business with the Jeffers girl. Lou shook his head and daydreamed about the past again.

That night, he had followed Ronnie. The other kid was having a party. When Lou had realized where Ronnie was headed, he quickly dashed down an alley and around the block. He cut his lights and parked right in front of the house. Ronnie'd parked across the street and had gotten out of his car. He'd run across the street, right smack into Lou who was leaning against his own hood.

Lou laughed again, remembering the look of disbelief on the kid's face. That look had turned to recognition, then panic within seconds! Ronnie never tried anything like *that* again!

A slamming door broke into Lou's reverie and he snapped back to the present. He felt truly sad about what he was going to have to do, but Ronnie'd been around too long. He knew too much. Yeah, the club was on the up and up, but it was the drug dealing and other things that Lou was worried about. Lou was really in deep—had been for years. That Escoba—really had him by the balls.

And so tonight Lou was not just going to kill Kate Jeffers in order to keep her quiet. He was going to have to kill Ronnie as well. After all they'd been through… He was going to miss having the kid around…

Lou shook his head again. He'd always been a softy—especially where Ronnie was concerned. He wished there was another way out, but…He sighed and he returned his attention to the terminal doors again.

Out of the corner of his eye, Lou noticed an emergency medical vehicle pull in and park. Absently, he thought he'd better make his shots count. He didn't need some overzealous medic rushing in to save their lives. If he had to go through with this, he couldn't make any mistakes!

CHAPTER 68

Kate

———— ● ————

Tuesday Evening

I rode with Whitaker to Hartsfield. He was acting strange—even for him. I knew he had wanted to get these guys for a while, but hey, I'd been after Mancini *myself* for thirteen years. I just hadn't known the man's name until this week.

Doug was even talking to himself. Man, he was a wreck. Then I thought about his wife again. Marcie had been shot in a situation similar to this. Poor guy, maybe that's why he was so jittery.

You know, he really is a super guy—he'd make a great husband for someone. In my mind I pictured him in the 'husband' mode. Yeah, he'd be okay.

I thought of Emily's parting comments, too. She had been eight when our parents died. I suppose she was young enough at the time to think that they didn't *want* to come back for some reason. Or maybe that she'd done something wrong that had caused their accident. And now she was concerned that I wouldn't return to her. Perhaps that's part of her problem now. Maybe that's why she couldn't tell me what happened that night with Ian. *Does she really not remember? Or is she afraid that I'll push her away somehow if she tells me the truth? Oh, man, what a mess!*

Finally we got to the airport and parked on the departure level. I tore my mind away from my sister and concentrated on our mission.

I gathered my purse and jacket. I adjusted the wire and small microphone that would keep me in contact with Whitaker. Stepping out of the car, I stretched for a minute. We tested the mic even though I could barely hear anything for all the jet engines. I hefted the suitcase out of the back seat. Man, money sure weighs enough! Lucky for me this was one of the roll-y bags.

Noise bombarded me. The floor of the parking structure vibrated. Even the air seemed to jiggle. And the smell of the airplane fuel made me feel sick. Couldn't possibly be my nerves! Glancing around and seeing nothing out of the ordinary, I braced myself and made my way into the terminal.

I entered, happy that the new parking lot went straight to Terminal F and I didn't have to take the long ride out to where the international flights depart. I wondered if the original plan had been for whoever picked up the money to immediately board a flight and leave the country.

Once inside, I checked with Whitaker again, via microphone, and slowly crossed the crowded terminal towards the security checkpoint. I didn't see anyone watching, but hoped that Carlos and Amy were somewhere close by.

Hopefully, they are the only *ones watching my every move,* I thought.

As I was looking around, getting my bearings, I had a weird sensation and a vision flashed before my eyes. It was of me and I was standing outside. Wind was whipping around and there were loud noises. Then, a small explosion, and things went black.

The vision only lasted a matter of seconds, but it was very disconcerting. "Lieutenant," I began, shaking my head to clear my thoughts. "I just had another vision."

"Kate," came Whitaker's voice. "You're breaking up…too much background noise…check back in a minute. Don't worry; Carlos is watching your back."

I glanced around nervously. *You shouldn't be like this*, I admonished myself. *You're going to look suspicious if you don't watch out, and blow the whole thing!*

Taking a deep breath, I managed to regain my composure as I walked through the International Terminal.

I was almost there when I noticed Carlos out of the corner of my eye. I hadn't even noticed him! A feeling of panic began to rise. *Och! What's he doing?* I silently screamed.

Then Carlos leaned up against the wall, looking totally nonchalant, and Amy, dressed in jeans and a Stanford sweatshirt, backpack in hand, started walking abreast of me. I realized I'd been holding my breath and slowly exhaled, *Duh…they're just following the plan.*

CHAPTER 69

Kate at the Drop

———— ● ————

Tuesday Evening

Things went smoothly because of the advance planning that Whitaker had done. I whipped through security in no time. The bag checker never even glanced up when she scanned my "carry-on" bag. I'm sure she's never seen that much cash—I know I haven't. When I got to the main part of the terminal, I looked briefly around (to give Amy time to catch up—I'd been walking way too fast!) and then headed to the escalator up to the Mezzanine Level. The welcoming agent had been briefed, just like the bag-checker. *Too cool!*

I entered the lounge, nodded to a couple people, and found a seat where I had a clear view of the escalators. I stowed my luggage next to me. My part was done...for a while, at least.

I briefly closed my eyes and tried to center myself while I waited for Ronnie to arrive and "do his thing". Then I did a quick scan of the area.

Pretty soon I saw him. I caught myself just before I broke out laughing; he was playing his part so well. Maybe he should take up acting! He came over to my seat with a bag of chips and offered me some. I shook my head, declining, and really did smile. Ronnie sat down close by and put his matching suitcase next to mine.

A few minutes later we took the escalator back downstairs together. Ronnie and I had swapped suitcases, very sneakily of course, and I followed him out into the main part of the terminal.

Everything was going so smoothly. It didn't dawn on me that this could be a bad omen. Then I remembered the vision I'd had as I'd entered Terminal F. I'd been so caught up with the ransom drop that I'd forgotten to say anything to Whitaker when we'd spoken again. I wanted to warn Ronnie to be careful, but there were so many people standing close by, that I couldn't say one word without hundreds of people overhearing! When had the place gotten so crowded? This could easily turn into a bloodbath if anything happened to go wrong! I began to sweat. Gross!

CHAPTER 70

Ronnie

Tuesday Evening

Ronnie and Kate walked through the main terminal. He rolled the suitcase along, full of bills. "Damn, this thing's heavy," he said to Kate who was dragging the empty suitcase behind her. They'd swapped cases upstairs in the lounge—no problem. He'd even had fun playing his part!

Once on their way to the parking garage, Ronnie let out a huge sigh—of relief, of fatigue. He was almost finished, but not quite. It was show-time again. He was going to have to "kill" the Jeffers girl. Lou'd be waiting at Prosciutto's for word from one of his other bouncers. He felt sure he'd been followed…just hadn't been able to spot anyone. The terminal had become so crowded. He prayed nothing would go wrong.

The plan was for Ronnie to grab a weapon from his car and "shoot" Jeffers as she walked away. She was then going to pretend to be dead while Lou's people looked on. Then the medics from the EMT vehicle were supposed to rush over and 'pronounce'.

Mancini's people would see the death transpire and would then call Lou and tell him that Ronnie had truly done the deed.

Ronnie was then supposed to take the suitcase to his car and head back to the warehouse on Monroe. He'd meet Emerson Bryant, the one who had demanded the ransom. Bryant would pocket whatever he was keeping for himself. Then Emerson Bryant and Ronnie would drop the rest, $400,000, back at Prosciutto's, where Lou was waiting.

Man, what a wad of money. Ronnie was surprised that Lou had allowed Bryant to run up such a big tab. Most of the dough was supposed to go to Nick Escoba—pay back for the drugs he'd smuggled into the country. Not a lot in today's market, but enough to really piss Nick off if he didn't get paid back real soon!

That was where the cops came in. They were going to surround Prosciutto's, especially the office and back stairs and arrest both Mancini and Bryant. Then they'd get the number of the account where Lou was going to wire the money—after that, it was just a matter of time before they could nail Nick Escoba!

As he and Kate made their way towards the exit, Ronnie wondered how the hell Lou'd gotten involved with Escoba and the drug trade in the first place. Any why? The club was doing well… Lou didn't *need* to do the illegal stuff. He was just small potatoes compared to some of the dealers. But there'd been that accident— maybe that's when he'd gotten involved. He'd have to ask Lou about that.

"Be real careful, Ronnie. Keep your eyes open," Kate warned as they approached the sliding doors. "I've got a bad feeling all of a sudden."

Ronnie slid a sideways look at Kate and groaned. Her "bad feelings" made him truly jumpy! He tugged the suitcase over the bumpy threshold and stepped outside.

That's when all hell broke loose! It seemed to happen all at once, but in slow motion as well. Ronnie heard three 'pops' from a weapon and the glass doors imploded. Shards flew in all directions. Ronnie jumped out and hit the floor of the parking deck, protected only by the suitcase. He scrabbled sideways, trying to get away from the opening and behind the closest vehicle. Another shot rang out, this one grazing his right leg, just above the knee. He yelped in pain, but kept moving.

He huddled behind the car, gripping his leg. He felt totally exposed and felt like a complete coward. "What the f___'s going on?" he yelled to Kate who'd managed to get to the other side of the entrance. He tried to figure out who the hell was shooting at whom. "You okay, Jeffers?" he shouted. He counted to ten, heard lots of voices, men and women, and then ventured a peek around the bumper of the car. *Good Lord!* he thought.

From out of nowhere, here came Glory like an angel of mercy. "Oh my god," she cried, marching towards him as though unconcerned that bullets had just been flying. "Ronnie—are you all right? Oh, crap, you're bleeding. Is it bad? Talk to me!" And she promptly fell into a heap in front of him, tossed the suitcase to the side as though it were empty, and gathered him to her breast.

"This is pretty nice," Ronnie said in a muffled voice. It's hard to talk when surrounded by double-"M" cleavage.

Glory pushed him away, annoyed, but laughing through her tears. "Cut it out. You scared the ever-lovin' crap out of me! Who the hell shot you? This wasn't supposed to happen like this. Can you walk? Where the devil's the life squad?"

Glory stuck her head up over the hood of the car, "Hey, y'all, I've got an injured man in here. He's bleeding like there's no tomorrow! Get over here and help!"

A uniformed officer came on a dead run. "Yes, ma'am. There's another guy injured on the roof—he's in bad shape—they were seeing to him first. They'll be right over."

Glory took another look. "Oh shit, Ronnie, I think it's your boss."

Ronnie pushed his way past Glory and the officer and hobbled farther out into the parking garage, dragging his leg along behind him. "I'll be okay," he called over his shoulder. "It's just a scratch."

Ronnie muscled his way through the medics who were indeed working on Lou. "You know this man?" asked one.

"Yeah...He's my..." choked Ronnie and he dropped to the tarmac next to Lou. How do you give someone like Lou a title? Boss? Friend? Surrogate father? The only one who'd ever given a damn about him?

"But *he's* the one who shot you..." started the officer who'd followed Ron out to the tarmac. His voice slowly died in his throat when he saw the obvious relationship between the two men on the ground.

Ronnie was kneeling on his good leg while sticking his injured leg off to the side. He'd scooted up next to the older man on the ground, and was cradling his head with both hands and his left knee.

"Lou...Lou! What are you *doin'* here? You're not supposed to be here!"

"Hey, kid," Lou answered breathlessly. "What happened? Where'd those shots come from? Nick said he'd get me...I guess he did. He got me good!"

"No, Lou, you'll be fine. Stick with me here."

"Nah, I'm a lost cause, kid. I'm sorry I had to shoot you, Ronnie. I didn't want to...you're like family to me. But I knew you weren't going to do what I said. I knew you'd let the girl live—and then I'd get sent up for sure. I'd never make it on the inside—you know that."

"Don't talk; just let these guys work on you, Lou. They'll get you patched up..."

"Get real, Ronnie...Look at me...there's nothing they can do and we all know it. Anyhow, I need to talk to you. I've got to tell you some stuff.

Gasping for air, Lou began, "You'll have to get some money to Escoba or he'll never leave you alone. Take it out of the club money...I've got enough in the account to cover it. Then stay the hell away from him...he's poison... Run Prosciutto's on the up and up—you'll do fine. Just think—if we make the newspaper with this shoot-out thing, business will pick up even more. You'll even have to hire some more help."

Lou started to laugh, but ended up with a racking cough that came from the soles of his shoes. Blood trickled from the corner of his mouth. "You're a good kid, Ronnie—always have been—you'll be okay without me…"

"Lou! No…Lou," Ronnie sobbed as Lou's head lolled to the side.

A medic stepped forward and said, "Sorry, son. Let us take it from here. We'll call the coroner. You can give the police your statement and make the formal identification. They'll let you know what happens next.

"Now, let's have a look at your leg. Looks like it just nicked you…let me help you over to the van…" and he pulled Ronnie away from Lou's body and guided the distraught man to the ambulance.

"What happened to Gloria?" asked Ronnie as he slumped onto the bumper of the vehicle.

"Who? Oh, you mean that big girl? She's sittin' on top of some guy over there."

Ronnie looked…and listened.

❈

They could hear Gloria's voice—even over the roar of the jet engines: "Who do you think you are, sittin' here in your fancy black car? You think just because you've got tinted windows that ol' Glory here can't see you shootin' at her friends? Wha's a matter with you anyway?

"No, I'm *not* gonna get offa you! Not till my friend the lieutenant here gets his cuffs on you! Now just lie still and let the man do his job!"

The medic grinned. "Who *is* she? And who's that poor fellow underneath her?"

Ronnie was getting a little woozy, but answered. "She's my new girlfriend." *Leave it to Gloria to bring down a guy like Escoba.*

"And that's Nick Escoba she's sitting on and giving hell to—he's a real bad dude from South America. I guess he must've shot Lou while Lou was taking a shot at *me*. Huh…must be why Lou missed."

CHAPTER 71

Westminster Terrace

———— ● ————

Tuesday Night

After hanging around the warehouse until after 8:00, Emerson knew there'd been some kind of trouble. Something had gone very wrong. He decided to head back to Arlington's house and wait for a call.

Penn Allister, Arlington, Janie and Officer Gomez were all there, standing in the library, too anxious to sit. Penn was wringing her hands. Arlington was staring out the window, hands clasp behind his back. The other two walked aimlessly around the room. No one had started a fire. It was too stuffy as it was.

"Well," asked Emerson when he came in, "what do we know?"

In an agonized voice Penn said, "Nothing! We haven't heard a word!"

"Wait…" Arlington said in a strained voice as he turned from the window. "Here come Lieutenant Whitaker and the others now!" He rushed to the front door to let them in.

Emerson kept his cool until Ronnie Walker walked in. "What are *you* doing here," he demanded.

"Who are you?" asked Penn Allister. Her voice raised an octave as she added, "And where's my baby?"

Ronnie smiled. "Let's let Kate explain."

"There have been several events over the years that, when combined, brought us together here tonight," Kate began. "First, let me introduce you, Penn Allister and you too, Janie, to those whom you might not know."

Introductions were made and everyone sat down.

"Now, allow me to try to sort this all out for you:

About 20 years ago, Emerson was injured in an accident. He got connected to Lou Mancini, who supplied him with pain-killing drugs.

Then, 13 years ago, Mancini and Nick Escoba, the South American drug czar, were in the car that ran my parents' car off the road. It was an accident, just coincidental, but Lou's name was in the hospital information, so the name Mancini was in the back of my mind. Escoba and he were the ones responsible for my mom and dad's deaths.

About 5 years ago Emerson ran up some debt with Lou Mancini. Arlington paid off Ronnie, Lou's man.

Emerson has since run up some *more* debts and Lou was pressing him for money again. Lou, in turn, was getting pressure from Escoba to pay *his* outstanding money.

"Then I started having visions. At first we didn't know how they connected, but now we do.

"My first vision was of my parents' accident. Escoba was driving and Lou Mancini was in the car. (Ronnie helped me make that connection.)

"My next vision was of you, Emerson. After some further investigation, we know how badly you were injured years ago at the frat house. We can all understand how easy it is to get hooked on painkillers and alcohol."

As Kate took a deep breath, Arlington cut in, "Emerson, no one ever told me what happened. Dad would never discuss that night with me. You know how he was… I'm sorry… I just… I didn't know."

"I blamed you," said Emerson in a quiet voice. "And then for years afterwards, I watched you get everything I couldn't—a wife, a great job, nice home…kids. Jane and Eddie were the kids I could never have!

"I couldn't take it. I started drinking and drugging more and more. I kept losing jobs. And I owed Lou all that money," he continued. "Last time I was in rehab, you told me you wouldn't help me anymore. I believed you. I'd have said the same thing if I'd been you. But I was in trouble again. I didn't know what else to do…" Emerson looked down at the floor, ashamed. "That's why I took Eddie…And now…I don't know where he is! I never meant for him to get hurt…I would never do that…I love the Kiddo. Family is all anyone has. They're supposed to take care of each other. I just wanted to get back at you for not being a good "big brother" to me all those years ago. And now…look what I've done! Penn. Arlington…I'm so sorry." And Emerson broke into muffled sobs.

Everyone in the room dabbed their eyes.

All at once a strange look came over Penn Allisters' face. She sprang from her chair and began walking towards Emerson. "Wait! Just a second! *You* took Eddie?" Penn Allister shrieked at Emerson, "*You!?*" She snarled like a wild cat. Arlington rushed to Penn and held her tightly by her shoulders.

"Come with me," he said and guided his hysterical wife from the room.

Everyone took a deep breath when Arlington closed the door behind them.

Janie scooted forward in her seat. She concentrated hard on the conversation and stared daggers at her Uncle Emerson.

Kate continued, looking pointedly at Emerson Bryant. "My third vision was of the warehouse. We now know that *is* where you kept Eddie. We're sure there was someone else involved, but so far we don't know who that person is. Maybe you'll tell us what we need to know, Emerson.

"But we *do* have some great news." Kate nodded to Lieutenant Whitaker, so he could finish.

"Ah, yes. The good news, Mr. Bryant." Whitaker cleared his throat and said, "*We have Eddie,* Emerson. He's fine."

"Eddie?"! Emerson snapped to attention. "Where? He's okay?"

"He's here. I'm sure Penn Allister and Arlington are with him right now."

At that news, Janie grinned and bolted from the room shouting, "Mom? Dad? Where are you?!...Eddie!"

"And we have the money," Whitaker continued. "That will go back to your brother.

"Lou Mancini is dead. Shot tonight by Escoba. And thanks to Gloria, Nick Escoba is behind bars.

"We've already spoken to your brother. Arlington's only interest is in getting some help for you—he's not going to press charges.

"Ronnie's agreed to testify against Escoba—to tell all he knows.

"Thanks to the detectives' hard work and Kate Jeffers' visions and help, everything has turned out all right."

❖

"Look..." cried Penn Allister, coming back into the library. "Look who's here...it's my baby."

She came in, her right arm around Eddie, her left around Arlington. Janie followed, all smiles.

EPILOGUE

Kate

———— ✸ ————

Wednesday, Very early in the Morning

Emerson Bryant is going to get the help he needs. Eddie will probably forgive his "favorite" uncle. With the love, support and understanding of his family, Emerson may make it to full recovery this time.

Ronnie and Glory...I left them comparing their respective rap sheets...and their tattoos. Will it last? Who knows?

Lieutenant Whitaker is already back at the station, hard at work on another case. I hope he calls me soon.

Joey was back at work Tuesday morning. Eddie confided in us about Joey's involvement...but nobody's saying a word.

Janie can't wait until her next writing assignment in English class.

Penn Allister and Arlington happily agreed to pay for Emerson's treatment. They might allow Jane and Eddie out of their sight... in a few years!

Me? My plans? I'm going to take my phone off the hook and sleep for a week.

I also aim to find out what happened between my sister, Emily, and Ian. There's something seriously huge going on there.

On top of that, I think our parents' deaths hit Emily harder than I'd previously thought. I want to be a better sister. I want to be available to give her whatever support she'll need during the next months or years.

And, of course, I'm looking forward to being the world's best aunt to David and Sarah's baby.

When I think about Lou and Ronnie, it reminds me that families come in all shapes and sizes. I know Ronnie will miss Lou. I don't want to have any regrets in years to come. I plan to spend more time with both my grandmothers. They won't live forever.

I think I'll start taking the stairs more often. Maybe not *all nine floors*...but? I kind of like being able to run all over the place and not find myself huffing and puffing.

And I'm going to learn to cook. Maybe start with something easy...Tzatziki Sauce?